I0736169

HIS GOLD PACK OMEGA

MIYO HUNTER

To Marie
Thank you for bullying me into writing this, LOL! Best writing buddy ever :)

Copyright © 2023 by Miyo Hunter

All rights reserved.

No part of this book may be reproduced in any form or by any electronic or mechanical means, including information storage and retrieval systems, without written permission from the author, except for the use of brief quotations in a book review.

CONTENT WARNING

HOLD UP! Is there anything I should be aware of as a reader?

This is an MF standalone, and it contains graphic depictions of violence, mature sexual situations, and death.

Attempted sexual assault and mentions of sexual assault (not between main love interests).

If you object to violent imagery, cursing and spicy scenes, this is not the series for you.
-xoxo Miyo

A GOLD PACK OMEGA

An omega who chooses not to go to the Institute within a year of perfuming.

Without the injection the Institute offers, their eyes turn gold, marking them as outcasts and a threat to society's safety. Nothing keeps them or their alpha offspring from reverting to violent roots.

Gold pack omegas are forbidden from having children, and are unprotected by many laws designed to keep omegas safe.

ONE
PANDORA

"Why would a girl like her ever choose to be gold pack? How does something like that happen?"

"Okay, the Delgado pack. Smash or pass." Sylvia shuffled her three large shopping bags to one arm, so she could toy with a curl in her hair.

"Pass." I bit the inside of my lip to hide a smirk. This was her third time bringing up the Delgado pack. They had to be her favorite.

"Seriously? Why? Those alphas are fine." Sylvia was pouting. Actually pouting, as if I'd just told her four-year-old self that Santa wasn't real, or that the winter formal was canceled.

Yeah, they were fine. Just like the last couple of times she'd brought up how attractive they were.

"I mean, most of them are hot. But that one red headed guy... he's kind of shrimpy."

"Panda! Are you talking about David?" Her voice hissed, as if we were saying something scandalous. "He has a lighter build, but he's still got at least a six-pack."

I was tempted to say that I doubted it. Or to even bring up that he'd gone to a gala event a few months back with a suit that looked *rumpled* at the sleeves. But Sylvia was saved from my teasing, when a sleek black car rolled up in front of us. It was the company car today, not the Mercedes.

Finally.

My driver was eleven minutes late—which wasn't like him. Henry was never late.

He could have at least texted me if there was traffic, or if he'd gone to get a coffee, but he'd left Sylvia and I stranded in front of the mall in radio silence. I had almost started to get worried, but Henry might be having a rough day or something. He had a real life, and more things to worry about than the pair of sixteen-year old girls that he was chauffeuring around.

"Hey, Henry? What's with the wait? Did your phone die or something?" I called out, as I buckled myself in, settling my bag at my feet, careful not to jostle the delicately wrapped tissue paper. I'd found the scarf that Mother had been eyeing. It was in Charisma's new spring collection. Silky, light. Perfect for her birthday. The sort of thing Mother would never buy for herself.

He didn't say a thing. Just stared straight in front of him, holding the steering wheel tight.

It was like someone had taken my friendly, middle-aged driver and replaced him with a robot.

An uneasy feeling stuck to the bottom of my stomach.

I tried to give Sylvia a *look,* to see if she'd noticed too. But she was just scrolling through her phone, not paying any attention.

The unease tugged at me, as I snuck glances at Henry in the rear-view mirror. He was wearing a mask. Which he did sometimes, when he was feeling sick... but I couldn't recall whether he had worn one when dropping us off in the morning.

I was feeling a bit like I was a heated teapot, with all of the steam running out. Nothing but hot water threatening to spill over.

The inside of me was boiling with anxiety.

But I didn't want to overreact and cause a scene. That was one way to ruin a perfectly good shopping trip. If word got back to my parents that I was having trouble with my driver, he could be reassigned and I didn't want to cost him his job. Not over one bad feeling.

I didn't speak up until Henry drove past my exit.

I plastered a wide smile on my face. Waiting for the moment that Henry admitted that he was tired today.

"Henry...?"

Nothing. It was like he didn't even hear me.

I cleared my throat, unsure, trying to catch his eyes. Was he ignoring me on purpose? "You... missed my turn."

TWO
MITEXI

The entire pack was huddled around the box. Inside, was the smallest orange kitten I'd ever seen looking back at us, meowing pitifully.

We'd just spent about an hour on a call getting the little guy out of a tree. But the people who'd called our department didn't even own the cat and they were gone before we'd finished carrying him down the ladder.

"What do we do with him?" Will crossed his arms, frowning.

"Little Fireball looks hungry. Doesn't he?" Chase was talking to the cat in a baby voice I'd never heard from him before.

"No. We are not naming him." I had to nip this in the bud. Once Chase got an idea in his head, he'd get all of the rest of the pack to join in. We did *not* have room in our apartment for a cat.

"There's a can of tuna in the back." Tycho pointed to the cabinet on top of the kitchenette.

Even Tycho? I'd thought that at least he would agree with me. But no, though Tycho kept a stoic look on his face, through the pack bond there was a spark of warmth.

"You didn't even want to get him out of the tree." I ran my fingers through my hair, exasperated.

"That call was a waste of our time. But that wasn't this little guy's fault." Tycho's eyes were fixed on the kitten, with a smirk on his face.

If even Tycho liked the cat, I was in danger of being overruled.

"This isn't our cat, we can't keep him. What if we find our omega and she ends up being allergic?" I refused to look in the box as the kitten mewed once more.

"Our omega is going to be perfect for us. She wouldn't be allergic to our cat." Chase was reaching out to the little kitten, scratching under his chin.

It *definitely* didn't work like that. While we could theoretically have dozens of scent matches, once we found one it would lock in, revealing that the omega was ours. Our destiny. Ours to love and cherish. We were waiting to submit our scent profiles to the Valentine Division at the Institute. Just needed to get some more money together. Our place worked, but would be tight once we found our omega. We had to offer her more than our small bachelor pad.

We needed a primary bedroom that could fit at least an Alaskan double-king bed. One with an oversized closet, with that memory-foam padded carpet. Everything had to be soft and perfect for our omega's nest. She deserved the best.

But the match had to do with pheromones and attraction; a combination of intention and desires. The scent match wouldn't magically take allergies into consideration. We couldn't risk keeping a cat.

"He doesn't seem to have anybody." Will pointed out. It was true. No one was taking care of the little guy. That didn't mean that it should be our responsibility.

If I left it up to the guys, they wouldn't see reason until the animal scratched all our stuff to shit.

But I wasn't a monster. I wasn't going to demand that we go dump the poor little guy off at the pound.

No.

We would do the responsible thing. Talk it over with the pack, and find some lonely kid to pawn the fluffy menace off to.

My thoughts were interrupted as alarms blared, signaling that we got a call. As we suited up, I didn't miss the unmistakable snap of a tuna lid, as Chase plopped the can into the box, before racing off to the fire truck.

Mentally, I was shaking my head. The guys were already getting attached.

The call was brutal.

An apartment complex had caught fire, with flames billowing out of multiple windows. The damage could be even worse than it appeared, just waiting for a draft to fuel the spread. The heat blasted all the way down to the street, making me sweat beneath my mask.

It was early evening, so at least not everyone was home from work. But school had let out not long before. There could be kids trapped inside.

We were running out of time.

One mother was screaming and pointing at one of the windows engulfed by flame. "—My son. On the fifth floor, he's twelve!"

"Ma'am, we are going to do everything in our power to get him out." Without taking my eyes off the flames. Silently calculating. It was a race against the clock. Enough for a primary search, going through rooms and marking them with an X.

"Fifth floor." I met Chase and Will's gaze. They could feel my hesitancy. I didn't shut down my side of the bond, letting them know the risk that they were facing.

For me, I knew exactly what I would do.

I was born for this. To face the fire. To pit my strength against flame and destruction. As long as I could save one life, it was worth it for me.

But I'd never ask that of anyone else. Much less my own pack. They deserved to know the full extent of the danger. Even if it meant I was taking on all the heat, alone.

Courage and resolve flashed through the bond back from them.

My pack bolted inside.

Forming teams, Will and Chase sprinted to the top—with their lighter builds, the two were the fastest on the squad. Honestly the fastest in the county. Through the bond, I felt the steady beat of Will's determination. It was a fierce rush, as all his gritty resolve pushed him forward. From Chase there was only single minded focus. They were the best shot that kid had.

Tycho and I swept through the lower floors. Chopping through doors and listening. Straining my alpha senses, for faint signs of life in all the chaos of flames through the crackling heat. Tuned into the bond the entire time.

Tycho watched the fire—poised to pull me down in case of a backdraft. Anytime we broke through a door or a window it changed the dynamic of the fire. He'd saved me before from a ball of flames as it raced along the ceiling, straight towards me.

Screams within one of the rooms demanded my attention. I slammed my ax into the door, hacking it open. Heat and flame billowed out, but I ducked through it. Following the sound of crying.

Inside a little girl sat huddled. All pigtails and tear streaks running down her cheeks.

I reached for her, but the kid just cried louder, pushing further into the room—that happened sometimes. With our masks on and surrounded by flames we looked like devils.

I didn't have time to worry about it. I grabbed the kid by her skinny arm, dragging her to me and slinging her over my back. Holding her by the legs, I scanned the room for anyone else.

Something in my gut nagged at me. Was there someone else in here? The squirming and screams of the kid weren't making this any easier.

"Keep looking," I shouted at Tycho. "I'll get her out."

I raced down the stairs and outside of the building.

By now, paramedics had arrived on the scene. Heading to the closest rig, I handed the crying kid off. Watching for half a moment as they assessed her, placing a non-rebreather oxygen mask over her little face.

I turned just in time to see the building buckle in on itself. Each floor crushing flat. The crash as it fell to the ground. Turning the building and everything in it into nothing more than flaming debris.

All I could hear was the echo of the crash, resounding through me. The quiet. As if the very world stopped, holding its breath. Freezing the chaos into a deafening calm.

Then the world restarted.

Sirens echoed through the streets.

Panicked onlookers pointed, screaming.

It was hard to make out anything beyond the ringing within my own head. The raging pain and whiplash. As if someone went straight into my mind, grabbing all the connections by the roots. Yanking them out.

That warm optimism, where Chase was supposed to be... it was gone.

I raced through my connection to Will—the most steadfast of all of us. Dependable. Found nothing at the end of it.

Reeling.

I dropped down, my knees hitting the pavement. Couldn't hold myself.

The raw void, left within me... as those ties shattered, one by one.

I knew what it was, the instant each one snapped.

From Tycho, I felt a brief flutter of fear. Then white hot agony —sharply cut off.

No.

Not wanting to put a voice to it. Not wanting to say it out loud. As if the simple rebellious act of ignoring it could stop it from being true.

It was the feeling of my pack bond breaking.

THREE
PANDORA

They kept me locked in a room barely larger than a closet.

No light came through except for the little sliver that shone under the door, and that never changed. It was just enough dim light to see murky outlines of things. Enough for me to tell that the bruises on my arms had started to fade.

I huddled in the corner of the room, running my hands along my arms to try to keep warm. It was so cold.

I had no idea how long it had been. Since I was kidnapped. Since the pack had jammed a phone against my ear, with Mother on the line, frantic. Cutting off the call in the middle of her telling me to just stay calm that they were coming for me.

All the hours blurred together.

But I preferred the dark to their footsteps. I cringed, pressing myself as tight against the walls as I could get. As if there was any way I could disappear into them, and escape.

All of those alphas, with their hard hands and bruising grips and cold stares.

I just wanted to go home.

My stomach was starting to hurt. Not because they were

starving me. The alphas would unlock the door and slide in plates of food once a day.

Despite the cold, my hands started to feel clammy. My head was pounding with a low ache. The pain in my stomach shifted lower. Cramping.

Something was wrong.

All at once, scent poured out in a rush.

What... was that?

The small space was soon flooded by the heady, feminine scent that was floral and sweet. It was as if someone had dumped a gallon of flower-based essential oils in here. But where was it coming from? There was no one in the room but...

Oh.

Oh, *no*.

"Not now," I whimpered. Pressing my hand against my mouth, desperate not to attract their attention. This couldn't be happening.

I always thought that I'd be a beta. Just one of the crowd, like everyone else.

Now was the worst possible time to find out... that I wasn't.

Not when the nearest alphas were all cold, hardened criminals. Men who'd already hurt me.

It was almost funny. How Sylvia and I used to gossip about what we'd do if it ever happened to us. I admit that I'd always secretly hoped for it. But I never thought...

Not like this.

I was perfuming because I was an *omega*.

The change wrought in my body was a pheromonal reaction—releasing a scent that would alert everyone to the transformation taking place in my body. Strong enough to draw in the attention of every alpha a mile away. Strong enough to put them into rut...

There was no way that the alphas who kidnapped me would

do anything. I mean, alphas were designed to be attracted. But they wouldn't want to risk their ransom money.

Right?

FOUR
PANDORA

"Panda, sweetie. I need you to really think about the choice that you're making right now."

I stared at my mother with dull eyes. Trying to figure out a way to put it into words. The effort it would make to have her hear me. It only made me feel more tired.

Everything made me feel tired.

Tomorrow would mark one year from the day I perfumed.

Since that kidnapping pack had zip tied my hands together and blind folded me. Since they dropped me off halfway in the middle of nowhere and left me there. Stranded for who knows how long. Until the screech of tires, the heavy footsteps. Until I was surrounded, once more.

Then too many hands reached for me. It didn't matter that at some level I could tell that these were my rescuers. Many of them were betas. Harmless. But I could smell the alphas among them. That strong masculine musk.

It's funny how that smell never used to paralyze my mind with fear.

"I know that it isn't something that you want right now. But you need to consider your future. Think of the kind of life you would have as a gold pack omega. That isn't something that you can take back." Mother was trying to keep her voice calm, even as her voice wavered. Once more I had her at the cusp of crying.

"I don't want to go." I know that it didn't make any sense for me not to go to the Institute. I knew that my choice was irreversible.

Tomorrow would mark the year, and without the injection, my eyes would go gold.

I'd heard it before. Over and over again. I'd heard nearly a year of it, from my therapist, from friends that came with their forced cheerfulness. Trying to shake me out of... whatever this was.

Nothing that any of them said changed my mind.

It didn't matter that society would see me differently. Gold pack omegas were at the bottom of the barrel. The omegas who had refused to go to the Institute. The ones who had spat at all of society's conventions.

I had never even seen a gold pack omega before. It wasn't polite to mention them in public. But I'd heard all of the rumors about them. People said they were promiscuous. Overfilled with scent, luring in alphas.

No one expected them to bond well.

None of the alphas I knew would ever go after a gold pack omega.

But they also could do whatever they wanted.

"Sweetheart, it wouldn't be safe. What if someone tried to dark bond you?" Mother stopped as I shook my head. We'd talked about all of this before. It didn't matter. I wanted to stay at home anyway. If I ever decided to leave, I could pay for protection.

Besides. I'd already tried the safe option. I'd been a good girl. Followed all the rules. None of that had stopped them.

"Don't you want to have your own pack someday?" Mother's voice grew softer, as her chin wavered.

This choice I was making, it was hurting her.

I didn't have the energy to care anymore. I knew that it was a bad idea. I knew how everyone would see it. But that didn't change a single thing.

Not when the thought of my own pack of alphas made me anxious. All those hands... touching me. I forced the thought down as bile rose in the back of my throat.

"I won't. I'm never going to want my own pack."

FIVE
MITEXI

The glare from the sun managed to pierce through the blinds. Growing too bright to ignore. I grabbed my downy comforter and pulled it over my face. Blocking everything out.

I only had a few days left of bereavement leave. I'd already gotten a voicemail from the mayor, asking for me to interview some new alphas. Fire fighting squads were always made up of bonded packs. Was he asking me to interview alphas to form a new pack?

I already had a pack.

I hadn't responded.

I'd held it together for the funerals, and was a gracious host when the next of kin came to the pack house. Sorting through the things that my pack brothers had left behind.

With every new possession taken away, I felt that my pack was ripped away from me all over again.

They were good men. Brave. I wasn't the only one that missed them. Their families deserved something to remember them as well.

It was the right thing to do.

As soon as all of them left, I walked through the patchwork of items left behind. The post-its on Chase's mirror, mentioning a new workout routine. Another with his morning affirmations.

I am successful

I am strong.

I am living with abundance.

I am grateful to be alive.

Without permission my hands moved, ripping the post-its down, all of them. Crumpling them tight. Until they were a wadded mess in my palm.

Shaking, I let them go. Falling to my hands and knees, I pulled open each post-it. Taking care to flatten them. I placed each little paper back where they had been on the glass.

When I found the list of Chase's affirmations, I smoothed it out carefully, reading through them once more.

Why couldn't he have made it?

I moved to place the affirmations back and paused, slipping the little bits of rumpled paper into my wallet instead.

Why couldn't I have given the kid to Tycho? Had him take her out to the rig?

There were traces of them all throughout the house. Not enough to feel like things were normal. Just enough to trigger my despair.

I refused to touch the food that they'd left behind, letting it rot within the containers.

They should have been able to come back. That food was never meant for me.

My bond ached like a phantom limb.

It was too quiet in my own mind, when before I could always feel a sense of how my pack was doing. It had been chaotic, always having the presence of all of them pulling on me. Depending on me.

The quiet was too loud.

Little paws walked across my still form, where I lay in my room. Only slightly heavier than a wet cotton ball. Fireball parked his little body in front of my face that was still covered in blankets. Letting out a plaintive cry.

The cat wasn't going to feed himself.

"Come here, little guy." I cradled the little kitten close to my chest. He really was tiny—barely bigger than the meat of my palm.

Slowly, I pulled myself up, looking to see if there were any other random tuna cans left around somewhere.

SIX
PANDORA

Five Years Later

I carefully placed the backings on my new stud earrings. Diamond. Mother sometimes looked away when I wore gold jewelry now.

Gold. Like the color of my eyes.

She liked to bring up how they used to be such a lovely blue. But she hasn't mentioned it recently.

That's fine. Saying it won't change anything.

I stepped out into the foyer, where Mother was waiting for me. She nodded approvingly at my ensemble giving me a tentative smile. "This is a big step. Your father and I are proud of you."

I wore a cross drop cable knit sweater with designer jeans. The outfit looked youthful. From what I could gather on social media, it followed the current trends. Thank God for online shopping. It stopped me from looking like a fashion-less hermit, despite the fact that I had rarely gone out in years.

On the outside I was lovely. The kind of woman anyone would love to get to know.

Inside I was a jumble of broken pieces, held together by routine.

I nodded, smiling as if everything was fine. Like I was actually as ready as all the time that passed said I should be.

"He has all the best recommendations. A letter from the mayor. An award for special services from the state. He even has first responder experience. You really couldn't ask for a better alpha to be your bodyguard."

All the air in the room tightened to a pinprick.

Breathing deeply, I gave myself a mental shake.

Hold it together.

I reached back to the part of me that was still locked away, sixteen again, huddled into the dark.

It's not the same alphas. It's only one man.

"You hired an alpha?" I asked quietly.

"Darling, there weren't any betas who applied for the position." Mother spoke quickly, as she watched my expression warily.

I couldn't ruin this for her.

Mother had been so excited, after I had told her I was finally ready to start going out once more. Ready to face the world. Possibly take on more of a public role in the family business. Father had even started to come out of his shell. He'd been so withdrawn, after everything.

I was ruining everything already, because I couldn't even hold it together when she'd even mentioned an alpha. I hadn't even met him yet.

I grabbed hold of the thoughts as they spiraled out of control. No. This wasn't *them.* I was safe, at home. I wasn't going to ruin this for her. Had to at least give the man a chance.

After the incident, Mother and Father went through a more rigid security check with all new potential employees. I was sure that they had additional screening measures in place for me.

Mother was still staring at me anxiously. I realized that she was waiting for a response from me.

"Okay."

It was always a longshot that I would be able to find a beta to apply for a protective position. It was an even longer shot that any beta I'd hired on as my bodyguard would be strong enough to take on an alpha.

I should have expected this.

I hadn't expected this.

But, if I met the guy, and his smell triggered me, I could always politely ask Mother to search for new applicants later. I probably wouldn't even have to. Mother would quietly take on all the preparations herself as I went to pieces. Same pattern as always.

This could still be my new start. I had to at least be willing to try.

"Are you ready to meet Mitexi?"

I couldn't reply. I merely nodded. Clenching my hands at my side to cover the faint shaking.

From somewhere behind me, I heard a door opening. Then heavy footsteps approached, stopping a few feet away.

I can do this.

I turned.

My throat went dry, and it had nothing at all to do with *fear.*

He was wearing a simple suit. Off brand, but well fitted. He was broad, and filled up the space around him with an energy that was magnetic. Dark haired with warm olive skin and a chiseled jaw. His eyes were a light gray like rain in spring. Who knew that such a subtle color could be fixed on me with a stare so intense?

He was quite simply the most handsome man I'd ever seen.

I had to tell myself to get it together for a completely different reason.

From this close, my mind was completely full of his scent—cardamom. A perfect mix of sweet with a hint of spiciness, like baking a crisp green apple.

The richness, the appeal of his scent... was this a scent match?

I'd heard that a scent match was like a shift within oneself, where the entire world became untethered, recentered with your mate's scent at the center. With an understanding that this was your match. Nothing and no one would compare.

He smelled amazing, but that wasn't what was happening here.

This couldn't be a scent match.

If it was, wouldn't he be saying something?

He was the first alpha I'd gotten close to in years, and his scent didn't make me want to break down in hives. It could be that my therapist was more right than I thought. This didn't have to mean anything.

Everyone was quiet. I realized that I had been silently staring at the man.

Mother was holding herself still with a fixed look of firm politeness on her face. A mask. Waiting for the moment that I'd inevitably crumble, and she'd be forced to swoop in and pick up all the pieces.

Well not today.

"Hi." I said.

Why did my voice have to sound so high and breathless?

I met one hot guy, and immediately reverted back into a stupid teenager.

"I'm sure you've been briefed on the details and nature of this job?" There I go. I've turned into some kind of walking dictionary. Sure. That's better than an airhead.

"Yes, ma'am."

Why did his voice have to be so deep that it rumbled straight through me? It was decadent. Smooth as truffles in dark chocolate.

Suddenly it didn't seem like the worst thing in the world to step away from Mother's protective wing and go into the world. And perhaps get to know Mitexi a little bit better.

"So you understand the intricacies of the assignment? With my status, I could be legally dark bonded. As the heir to the Delano business and fortune, there will always be people tempted to use me. Do you think you'll be able to protect me?"

"I won't let anyone hurt you." From him, the words sounded like a solemn vow.

For the first time in years, I believed it. He could keep me safe.

Mother stared at me, her mouth parted in surprise, as I stepped out of the house with him. As if it was nothing. As if it wasn't the first time I'd willingly left in years.

Mitexi was huge, but something about him didn't scare me.

He seemed like more than enough to take on any threat that wanted to hurt me.

SEVEN

MITEXI

This new job was going to kill me.

I was supposed to be looking after some rich socialite. Protect her as she went to the mall, and grocery shopping or whatever she needed to do.

Seemed perfect. Low stress. Low responsibility.

I couldn't keep burning through the pack savings. Had to do something while I decided what I was going to do with the rest of my life.

Plus the pay for this position was obscene. On paper it was a sweet gig. Keep some bratty twenty something year old safe, and make enough to keep up on payments to the pack house.

The first moment I saw her, I went rock hard.

Looking into her sweet eyes, I knew that I was in over my head. They were the exact golden shade as her hair that fell in waves. Full lips. High cheekbones that belonged on the cover of magazines. Pandora looked angelic.

Poised and sophisticated.

With a body that was luscious with full curves I was itching to touch.

It was a fucking good thing that these pants were loose. The family was watching me like a hawk. I tried taking deep breaths and that made my situation worse.

Her *scent*. It was exquisite.

She smelled goddamn amazing. I don't think that I've smelled something in my entire life that was so fucking good. Delicate and floral... was that lillies? With another scent that was sweet and smooth, like vanilla with a hint of spiciness. Luxurious.

Whatever it was, it smelled like a perfume I couldn't afford. Out of my league.

Get your head out of your ass, she's your boss.

I was resigned to ignore my attraction to her.

"Where do you want to go?" I asked her, as I followed her into the back of her luxury car. A driver with a neat cap and white gloved hands positioned exactly at nine o'clock and three o'clock waited for her to tell him our destination.

She didn't say anything.

After she buckled herself into her seat, Pandora went completely still. Like she was a deer caught in the spotlight.

I'd thought that she was just considering where she wanted to go, until I noticed that her hands were shaking.

Her gaze was far away. Whatever she was seeing or feeling, it wasn't here with us.

It took me a minute to recognize the symptoms; she was right in the middle of a panic attack.

"Hey," I crouched in front of her, making myself as non-threatening as possible. Reverting back to my first responder training. "What do you need?"

Pandora shook her head. Her mouth was parted, and she was struggling to breathe, taking in air with short irregular breaths.

"Easy now. Breathe with me." I took a deep breath in, encouraging Pandora to do the same. Breathing out deeply, my eyes on hers the entire time. "That's it," I encouraged, taking another breath in, as she mimicked my inhales and slowed her breaths down.

After a few minutes, her breathing went back to normal and the first thing she did was flush bright red and look away from me.

"I'm sorry." Her voice was soft, but bitter. As if she was angry at herself.

Why was she blaming herself for having a panic attack? It wasn't a choice.

"You have nothing to apologize for." I tried to make eye contact with her. Communicate without words that this wasn't her fault.

Pandora stared resolutely at the floor, avoiding my gaze as moisture gathered at the corner of her eyes. She sniffed, blinking rapidly to hold away tears.

"Don't tell my mother. I don't want her to worry about me," Pandora said in a small voice.

"I'm here for you. Not anyone else." I dipped my head down, so that I was in her field of vision.

Finally, she met my gaze.

I expected her to be this pampered little rich kid. One who wouldn't demean herself by talking to me, but as Pandora's eyes met mine, she bit her lip.

This shy, delicate dove wasn't anything like I expected. I was bracing myself for someone who disrespected me, or ignored me. Not this.

"Do you still want to go somewhere?" It was fine if she didn't. Panic attacks were emotionally exhausting.

Pandora paused for so long, I wasn't sure if she was going to answer. Before she slowly nodded. "Let's go to the Pineford Mall."

I kept on drifting closer to Pandora, wanting to grab her hand.

This is not a date. She's my boss.

I might have been new at being a bodyguard, but even I knew that it wasn't professional to lust after my client. My brain just wasn't getting the memo.

I couldn't help being drawn to her. But I wasn't the only one.

It was early afternoon, on a weekday, so the mall wasn't particularly crowded. Most people were at work. Anyone shopping now had to be retired, or a bored housewife.

Wherever the two of us walked, people looked at Pandora.

At first, I thought that they couldn't look away from her because she was so attractive. But the stares of the people around her would linger on her golden eyes. Eyes that revealed her status as a gold pack omega.

Pandora showed no sign that she noticed them. But whenever a man stared more blatantly, she tended to move closer to me.

That was fine. That was what I was here for.

But honestly...

It was awakening something possessive in me. A feeling that had no business being there.

Mostly Pandora was window shopping, slowly drifting by each store, quietly taking in each outfit in the display, before moving on to the next. She stopped by one store, hesitating.

It was one of those stores that I would walk by, immediately dismissing it as too expensive. Something about the modern quality of the furniture inside, and the gold lettering. It all screamed that everything was out of my price range.

Pandora stepped inside.

I followed Pandora in, a few steps behind. Watching for any danger, but also trying to give her space. Pandora crossed the store, heading directly to a shelf full of purses.

There weren't any other customers. The entire boutique was completely empty besides the two shopkeepers.

One perked up as soon as she saw us. A young woman with stylish make-up walked directly over to me, with a wide smile. "Can I help you with anything?"

I shook my head, eyes on my surroundings.

I doubted that my suit was nice enough to make anyone believe that I could afford anything in this store.

Despite saying I didn't need any help, she lingered. Out of the corner of my eye, I vaguely noticed her leaning her shoulders back so that her chest was on display, in her sleek and form fitting designer apparel. It also made her name tag jut out, displaying 'CLAIRE' engraved in silver.

Was she flirting with me?

I ignored her.

The effect of her chic application of makeup was ruined by the sour expression she made when she saw Pandora. She stared blatantly at Pandora's eyes.

"That purse is eight thousand—" She called out.

"I don't need to know the price." Pandora cut her off. She didn't make eye contact with the woman. Examining something on the leather instead. The quality of the stitching or something.

"If you aren't planning on buying anything, you shouldn't touch that." Claire snapped.

Pandora made no sign of hearing a single word, besides the fact that her plush lips flattened. Then she quit examining the purse, crossing the store to bring it to the front, to the other shopkeeper. "These come in white, sable and red?"

"Yes... were you interested in one of them?"

"I would like one in every color." Pandora pulled out a sleek black credit card, handing it over.

"Yes of course." She ducked behind the register, pulling out a fancy shopping bag—a gold one with rope handles. Hurrying to the back of the store, and coming back with three bags, wrapping each neatly in tissue paper.

"I bet you twenty that her card's going to get declined," Claire muttered in a voice that wasn't quite low enough.

Her coworker paused for a moment, but otherwise acted as if she had not heard a thing. Instead, ringing up each bag on the register, and sliding Pandora's card for payment.

"Thank you for shopping with us, your receipts in the bag." She handed back the card and shopping bag, with a wide smile.

Pandora accepted them with a nod, taking a step away. Until she was directly in front of Claire.

"You get paid on commission, correct?" Pandora said mildly, in a tone that suggested that it wasn't really a question. "Today isn't your lucky day."

I wanted to pay for the food, my fingers automatically drifted to my pockets to get my wallet, before I remembered.

This girl is richer than God, and my paycheck comes from her regardless.

More importantly. This wasn't a date. I was working.

It had been a while since I'd gone out and gotten mall food. It had been a while since I'd gone out at all, in all honesty.

Besides, as soon as Pandora asked me what I would like to order, and I mentioned the chicken at the kabob place, she whipped out her fancy black credit card before I even had a chance to offer.

If I'd known she was going to pay, I would have said something cheaper, like a pretzel.

Once we sat down, I kept an eye out, especially for other alphas. Wouldn't let any of them come near her.

Then I noticed Pandora gazing down at her food

If I hadn't spent the morning with her, I would have assumed she was intentionally ignoring me. But no.

Now I doubted that. Pandora was probably just shy. Didn't know what to say to me.

"The way that you put that shopkeeper in her place. That was hilarious." I tried some small talk.

A small smile lit up on Pandora's face.

I smiled back at her.

My girl had some fire in her after all.

Stop. She's not your girl.

I went back to my meal, pulling the wrapper off my straw, and pocketing it.

"What's that for?" She asked, looking in the direction of the trash I just placed carefully in my suit pocket.

"Oh. This is for my cat. He likes to play with this kind of stuff." I felt inexplicably guilty, revealing the existence of Fireball. Which didn't make any sense. What did I have to feel guilty about? "You aren't allergic by any chance?"

"Me? I'm not allergic to cats. I'm only allergic to kiwi."

I swallowed the lump in my throat... *Chase.* Who believed that his omega couldn't possibly be allergic to their cat. Chase, who would eat anything. Except kiwi, for some weird reason. But I was the big idiot who had told him that scent matches didn't work like that.

She's not yours.

She's your boss. She's not even your scent match. Pull yourself together.

But if she wasn't, why did she feel so perfect?

EIGHT
PANDORA

Mother was hovering as soon as she got me alone.

"How did it go? Things went alright?"

I nodded. Trying to keep things casual. As if this wasn't the first time in years I'd left the home without her or Father. Like things were back to how they used to be, when I was an independent young lady, able to go off on my own without fear.

"It didn't bother you that he's an alpha?"

I shook my head, as I carefully looked over my new purchases. I'd been eyeing those purses online for months. The one tricky thing about online shopping was being able to tell how they would feel in person. Sometimes it took holding something in your hands to see if it felt like it belonged. As soon as I picked up the purse, I knew that it was mine.

"Because I just got an application in from a beta, so if you'd really rather have a beta as your bodyguard—"

"No," I said. Only realizing that I spoke too quickly, when Mother looked away to hide a smile.

Being around Mitexi almost made me feel like I was my old self again.

I don't know what it was about him. Every other alpha I'd gotten close to caused me to break into panic attacks. I'd get hives from just the thought of being close to them. The thought of their hands on me, made me feel like I was breaking even further apart. Like their hands were all covered in mucus, that their touch would stain me. Marking me in a way that everyone would be able to see.

But then there was him.

It wasn't that he made me feel the opposite of what alphas did. He felt like the spring breeze that cools away all the sweat, lifting me up. Freeing me from thoughts I hadn't realized were dark until his presence shone through. When he smiled at me, I felt it warm through every inch of my skin. Comforting all the broken pieces of me that I thought would never be whole again. Awakening parts of me that had long been asleep.

He felt right.

Which wasn't right.

He was my bodyguard. Of course he was keeping me safe. That was his job, and he just happened to be good at it.

Maybe I should just be happy about this. If I could fall for one man, that could mean that someday, I might be able to like another one? Maybe I didn't have to spend the rest of my life alone.

But the thought of being with anyone other than Mitexi filled me up with that same dread.

Late at night I tapped out several messages to him, erasing each one. Finally settling on something that I hoped sounded casual.

> Me: Hey, just letting you know, you have the week off. Starting on the third.

Immediately I saw the three dots on the bottom of my phone. I felt giddy, like bubbles fizzing through freshly poured soda, threatening to overflow.

Mitexi: Oh? Planning something fun without me?

I bit my lip; I just couldn't help it. Was he trying to be sexy? Whatever Mitexi was doing it was working.

The man was seduction in human form.

Other alphas made me cower away, but there was just something about him. I didn't know what it was. But while other alphas always seemed like a threat, his strength felt like safety.

I scrambled to come up with a message.

Me: Nothing like that. Just my heat.

I groaned after I hit send. Why did I have to mention something like my heat? Damn it. That was something so personal, and so biologically out of my control. Why did I have to blurt it straight out when I'd spent the last ten minutes carefully crafting the perfect vague message to send out to him?

...Why was he taking so long to respond? I watched the three dots on the bottom of my screen. Clenching my phone so hard that my knuckles were turning white.

Mitexi: Of course. I'm sure that you'll be needing privacy with you and your heat partner. But if any emergency comes up, please don't hesitate to reach out. I'll be sure to keep in close contact in case of any emergencies that may arise.

A pit dropped in the center of my stomach. *Heat partner?* Did he think that I was contacting some service to get over my heat? Hiring some random alpha to fuck me? Just the thought of it caused bile to rise in the back of my throat. I hadn't even looked twice at an alpha... not until he'd come along.

And was it me, or did this message seem a lot more formal than previous texts? I swear, his messages always seemed borderline flirtatious. Why did I suddenly feel like I'd messed up whatever it was that the two of us had between us.

> Me: No, lol

My frantic fingers hit send before I even had a chance to finish my thought.

> Me: Just me and my heat blockers...

That and gratuitous use of my favorite rabbit toys. I might get carpal tunnel syndrome decades early, but at least I wasn't under the control and mercy of some unknown alpha.

For my first heat, Mother didn't know what to do. She'd scheduled something like a professional heat partner and I'd gone into a panic attack so bad I'd nearly needed to be hospitalized.

> Him: That sounds painful

I looked away from my phone screen, screaming at the tears building in the corner of my eyes to mind their business and leave me alone. No one really acknowledged the emotional impact that the lack of a partner had on an omega. More than just the physical, omegas were hard wired to seek out an alpha. It was programmed into our biology. The blockers helped suppress the physical brunt of it, but nothing out there could take away the neediness of the omega within me. The omega telling me that no. It shouldn't be this way. I was violating my nature, choosing to lock myself away.

So unwanted.

So alone.

...better than being under their control.

Me: I'm used to it

I replied, brushing the back of my knuckles against the wet streaks on my cheek angrily.

Shaking my head.

I was fine. No matter what Mother and the rest of polite society might say otherwise. It was better this way.

Him: Well, my previous offer still stands. If you need me during your heat, don't hesitate to text me

Oh. My. God.

I bit my knuckle to hold back a squeal. Did that mean what I thought it meant? I could feel my whole face flushing red hot. Was Mitexi... was he interested in me?

The two of us weren't a scent match, but was he hinting at more?

Was he saying that he would be interested in helping me out with my heat?

My jaw dropped as butterflies rioted with my stomach.

I might have thought about it once or twice. Or more times than I was willing to admit. What it would feel like to have his luscious lips on mine.

What it would feel like if he was more than just my bodyguard.

I should say something back that was cool and seductive. Something that would have him drooling over me, like I was already swooning over him.

Me: Thank you :)

I didn't know what else to say.

I wanted to be that cool seductress. I wanted to know what I could say to lure him in. Let him know that yes I was very interested in whatever he had to offer.

Maybe that might have been me. Once upon a time.

But this version of me? After everything?

A cheesy thank you and a basic smile emoji ended up being the best that this broken heart of mine could manage.

NINE
MITEXI

I couldn't help but grit my teeth when I first saw the text that Pandora was getting her heat.

The thought of some other alpha having her made me want to gouge the fucker's eye out. My blood raced through my veins, as I saw red.

She's not yours.

Every day that went by those words meant a little less. The fact that getting too close to her would end up leaving me without a job, became a minor concern. None of that mattered as much as all the ways I could make a smile light up her sweet face.

I groaned at the thought of Pandora during her heat. As desire raced through my veins.

As my heart pounded for her. As I pictured what she would look like with her head thrown back, back arched. How she would feel around me as she took my knot.

I needed to get myself under control. It wasn't fair to anyone that I was having all these fantasies featuring her, Pandora included.

This was a job. I couldn't keep moping over a woman who was never meant to be mine.

Staying at home to drool over my boss—and how she was currently in heat—wasn't a good plan for my mental health. I decided to take a page out of Pandora's book, and head over to the mall.

It was different, heading there out of my bodyguard uniform. Passing by the luxurious brand name stores that Pandora gravitated to, and instead walking over to stores for the common man.

I was shopping for the first time in years.

I meandered along the same paths that Pandora normally took, and tucked into a corner was a store called Pet Emporium, with an incredibly tacky cartoon rendition of a smiling goldfish, a parrot and a kitten. I had to check it out.

Walking through the corridors, I couldn't help scanning the shelves for new treats for Fireball. Yes, the giant fur ball had everything that he needed. But he'd gotten me through a lot. With the salary that this new gig was paying, I could get him something special as well.

I meandered over to the cat section. Quickly passing over the selection of catnip. Fireball was a good upstanding cat-citizen and I was not going to support him in acquiring a drug addiction.

The dangling toys on a rope were an immediate no. I knew from experience that Fireball would get too excited by any toy like that and would try to run from me to eat the string. I ended up grabbing two packages of cat toys, trying to decide between the fake mice and feathered balls in neon colors. Was Fireball more likely to play with one of these sets? Or was he more likely to be interested in the box that they came in?

"Excuse me, are you Fire Chief Lee?"

My hand tightened on the boxes of cat toys, denting plastic. I tried to force myself to relax, even as I steeled my public persona to show nothing.

I turned around, schooling my expression to stay blank. Hoping to God that this wasn't one of the people from *the* fire. There were too many lives lost in that building that day. It wasn't just me that lost my pack. Whole families were ripped apart. People had lost their kids when that building went down.

I turned to face a wide-eyed kid. No one I recognized. He had freckles across his nose and braces with green bands—which I could clearly see because he was gazing at me in open mouthed surprise.

In response, I nodded slowly.

"You saved my sister's life. You're her hero."

I blinked in surprise, trying to get a closer look at him. Tried to see some resemblance, but my mind couldn't drag up anything distinct beyond the horror of the building falling. The echoes of pain... the last moments of connection in my bond.

"Could I take a picture with you? I want to send it to her."

I nodded automatically, without stopping to think about it. The kid stood next to me, holding his phone out angled at the two of us. I tried to make a smile, but my upturned mouth resembled a grimace more than anything pleasant.

"Thank you! My sister tried to send you a thank you letter. But we couldn't find your contact information at the fire department?"

It was hard looking at that smiling face, and admit the truth to him. "I'm not working at the department right now."

"Oh," the kid's nose scrunched up as he considered my answer. "But you're going to go back?"

"Yeah, maybe." I placed the cat toys back on the shelves, needing to get out of there. "It was nice meeting you."

It was the same question that I'd heard over and over again. After what everyone considered an appropriate mourning period, I got the weekly calls from my mother. Voicemails from the Mayor's office. Though the frequency of contact had slowed down, the question still remained. Unanswered.

So when are you going to go back to the fire department?

My problem wasn't with the work. Though my last call had shown without a doubt the dangers of the profession. No. I enjoyed the adrenaline of it. All of the dangers of working with my hands against the flames. Breaking through buildings and barriers to save people.

Fire squads always formed a pack.

I already had a pack.

How would I have gotten through training without Chase's relentless optimism? What would my work ethic have been if I hadn't worked for years right beside Will and his tenacity? Tycho. The man who I'd gotten closer to than anyone else in my life. He was brave, and he was gorgeous. More than anything, he was unshakably loyal.

These men were not replaceable.

They were more than brothers to me. I spent years feeling surges of every single one of their emotions. It was the four of us against the forces of nature. Ready to take on anything and build our futures together.

There was no way in hell that I could ever dream of opening myself up to a trio of strangers. Sharing pieces of myself in ways that only my pack had ever seen.

I couldn't do it.

I wouldn't do it.

This time around, the little office in the institute was a far more solemn affair. The last time I'd been here, I hadn't been alone. The room had been brimming with excitement. The four of us were ready to start the rest of our lives.

This time around, the doctor took his stethoscope from around his neck, placing it on his table. He pushed his glasses up the bridge of his nose, as he sighed. "Are you sure about this?"

I held out my hand for the little paper cup as my response. I took the little blue pill inside dry, ignoring the glass of water placed on the table. As soon as the pill hit my stomach, energy hummed through me. A dull reverberation—a shadow of the pull, the connection forged when the bond was opened between my pack brothers.

Which made sense, as now I was closing the bond.

What would they think of me now?

Yes, I was closing out the part of me that was able to bond. But I think my brothers would understand. After sharing that connection with them, it felt like a violation to rip everything back open and share the same things I'd shared with anyone new.

Though a part of me recognized that they might want me to move on, they'd understand why I couldn't do it.

It would be like completely erasing them.

I'd faced the emptiness inside of my own head for years now. But it had never before felt so... permanent. My designation was officially changed. The registry would update in 24 hours and I will officially be Silver Status. I'll legally be a lone wolf.

After my appointment, I didn't know what to do with myself. It wasn't that I regretted my choice; I'd made the choice that I could live with. But my appointment at the Institute made the reality I'd been ignoring real... all of the emptiness. Everything was so official.

Even though I wasn't needed, I found myself lingering near Pandora's home. Sitting in my car, just killing time. She was right at the start of her heat. Wouldn't need me for another couple of days. Maybe even a week. I knew all of that, but I just needed to be near her.

My phone pinged again and again with rapid fire texts.

No one ever texted me anymore. No one but Pandora. These texts weren't her typical style. She'd write a paragraph at a time, all with the correct grammar and punctuation.

She was texting me... during her heat.

After I practically propositioned her like an idiot.

The thought had me yanking my phone straight out of my pocket to read the series of texts there.

Pandora: Mitexi are you around?

Pandora: I can hear someone outside of my room. It sounds like they are trying to break in.

Pandora: I'm scared

TEN
PANDORA

It was only a soft clink at first. A high metallic sound that I could hear over the low buzz of my vibrator.

I could have dismissed it, easily enough. But I'd learned the hard way not to ignore my gut intuition. I powered my toy down to the lowest setting, laying it on my bed. Ignoring the immediate pulse of need that raced through the entirety of my lower body— the blockers helped numb the hormones, but nothing could erase them entirely. Well nothing other than a surgical procedure that would essentially leave me sterilized and with dozens of medical ramifications restricting my quality of life.

I stared intently in the direction where I'd heard the sound. Looking for whatever it was that had made the noise.

I'd already been looking at the approximate location. That was the only reason why I saw the slow and silent turning of my lock.

For one horrifying second, I stared at it in shock. Frozen. Immobile. No one was supposed to come into my heat room.

Inside my own mind I started screaming. Telling my useless body to move. Move. Just fucking move. I grabbed my phone off the side table, and my shaking hands managed to send out some quick messages to Mitexi.

It was all I had time for before the door—which was supposed to be double locked, and the corridor monitored by our security team—swung open.

A man walked in. Tall. Hulking and horrible. He shut the door behind him, and I heard the familiar click as the lock re-engaged.

I was laying in my bed, with my vibrator still going off somewhere by my legs. Completely naked from the waist down.

I'd never seen this man before. Hadn't seen him but knew immediately from the smell that he was an alpha. The musty stench of his pheromones assaulted me from the moment he'd stepped through the door. Like rotten marmalade that had been left out and rolled around in the dirt.

Was he someone who worked at my house? What the hell was he doing in here? My parents ensured that if we had any alphas on staff, they were warned to stay away from me.

I rose up, ignoring the ache in my lower belly. Ignoring my own nudity.

A feeling of numbness settled over me like someone had cracked an egg that was oozing over my mind. I pressed my fingertips against the safety panel installed just over my headboard. Inside I was ice. Moving my numb mind and forcing my unfeeling fingers to reach inside as the panel hummed open.

The man held his hands up, to show that he was unarmed. Walking slowly towards me, pretending that he was harmless and had any right to be here.

Like I couldn't tell the difference between caution and the steady walk of a predator.

I pulled my glock out of the safety panel. Pointing it steadily at him. "Don't come any closer."

"There, there sweet thing. You don't want to do that." His voice was oily smooth. Like syrup poured over gravel. I didn't trust it for a second.

The hours of practice paid off as I was able to seamlessly flick off the safety, resting my shaking finger steadily against the trigger.

"I'm an associate with your father. We've met before." He took a short step closer, as if I wasn't pointing a gun at him. "My name is Daniel."

"I want you to go." Had I met him before? It didn't matter. I didn't want him anywhere near me. Now. When I was vulnerable.

I wish Mitexi was here.

I shooed the thought away, like I already had dozens of times since my heat started. He wasn't here. This was mine to deal with.

"Is that what you really want? Omegas aren't meant to be alone. I can help you."

He took a slow step closer. His gaze trailed up and down my body. Tracing the outline of my silhouette, all the contours of my body were visible through my thin pajama top. Taking in my bare thigh, his gaze zeroed in on the blonde curls nestled in between my legs, glistening with slick, then his eyes snapped back to my face.

All the cold within me was replaced in an instant with white-hot anger. How dare he? How fucking dare he? He and every single alpha out there who assumed that they knew what was best for me. Since I was biologically receptive to alphas, that meant that I must want anything to do with *him*.

"You don't really want to kill me." Daniel's voice was deep and gravelly and full of undeserved confidence.

He was wrong. It was all I could think of. In my mind I pictured it over and over again. That twitch of my finger. How his head would burst into pieces like an overripe melon, painting my heat room with the red of my triumph over him.

Even now. Even armed, why couldn't I just move? All it would take was the smallest twitch of my finger and then all of my problems would be over.

Daniel took another step, rapidly eating up the space between us. My heat room was standard sized, but this was the first time it had felt so small. I wished for it to be as long as the Great room. Wished that I could pile all that missing space back between us.

The entire world was nothing but the metal against my index finger. All the freedom, all my piece of mind was centered on that little bit of muscle. All it would take was the smallest twitch. If I could just get my finger to move.

I kept on adjusting my aim, pointing it directly to his head. Then lowered it slightly to his torso. Anywhere. I could have pointed it anywhere. Just pull the trigger. I'd shoot him again and again if I had to.

He kept up his slow approach, until he was much too close. Until the stench of rotted marmalade was all over me, so close that it was pressing into my skin. It didn't matter where I shot him, I just had to fucking do it already.

I pulled the trigger, aiming straight for his heart. Only... pulling back against the metal of the trigger, wasn't working. It made the faintest clicking sound as if it was stuck somehow. But how? I was sure I was shooting exactly like I'd done in training.

In a whip fast movement, Daniel snatched my glock, ripping it out of my numb fingers. Jerking my gun away from me.

I'd been disarmed just like that.

Even after weeks of self defense training, following all the procedures, doing everything right.

A horrified whimper escaped past my lips as it hit me. The fact that I was a gold pack omega. The fact that I was in heat. That I had no legal protection to whatever this awful smelling alpha wanted to do to me in my own home.

He shushed me, as he placed my glock on the ground, kicking it to the far corner of the room. Where it was as useful to me as a wad of chewed up gum.

As he pressed his lips against my neck in a soft kiss, my vision began to swim. My eyes were thick with tears, and my arms started to shake.

No. I didn't want this.

I was just a kid before. I told myself I'd never let this happen again.

Why hadn't I shot him? Why wasn't I strong enough to just kill him?

After all the practice and everything.

Even armed.

Why wasn't I strong enough to do what it takes to protect myself?

"Don't worry, lovely." Daniel's hot breath was on me, puffing against my cheek. "This isn't going to hurt one bit."

The words rolled through me, spreading fire to each and every one of my nerves. Waking up every inch of me that was frozen. From the pit of all that helpless rage, I screamed. Screamed as I raked my nails against his cheeks, pushing away. I ran to the corner, where this sick fucker had kicked my gun.

"Shit." Daniel cursed softly.

I heard his loud footsteps pursuing me, over the hammering of my own heart. Gaining on me. As I moved faster than I ever had before.

A bang like a shot rang out across the room.

"What the hell?" Daniel looked back in the direction of my door.

Another sickening crack burst across the wood. Loud as a battering ram.

Ignoring the distraction, whatever it was. I dove for the gun— only to be yanked back by my midsection. Momentum pushed me forward as my fingers trailed across the floor. Close enough to my gun to briefly touch the metal; before I was yanked back, falling to the ground with a thud.

All I knew was panic. Behind me the rattling explosive blows shook the door. In front of me about three inches away, my gun. I scrambled, reaching for it. Before rough hands pinned me down. I frantically twisted my arms over my neck. Over my shoulders. Over every inch that I could touch. I had to protect myself. Shield myself.

There'd be no going back if he managed to dark bond me.

Daniel pulled my hair back, yanking my head up. I tried to resist, to break free from him, even as I could feel my hair ripping at the roots.

But I was too late.

Once more, Daniel's mouth was on my neck, this time with the bite of teeth. Pinching against me, breaking through. I could feel the dark intent behind his lips, scalding my skin.

No.

Please no.

Daniel's weight as well as the foul and wet press of his mouth was ripped away from me.

I scrambled away, grabbing my glock and swinging around to point it back—just in time to see that Mitexi had somehow broken in and was straddling my attacker, punching him in the mouth so hard that it cracked, dislocating his lower jaw. Scattering a handful of teeth across the floor.

I'd never seen Mitexi like this before, his whole face flushed, and rage burning in his eyes. His knuckles split open and poised over my attacker.

It wasn't until his eyes snapped to mine, and his nostrils flared that I finally noticed.

I'd always found his scent luxurious. Cardamom—a complex blend of sweet and spicy that smelled more than anything like the warmth of a baked apple taken straight out of the oven. With deep earthy undertones. Masculine and delicious.

His scent had always been appealing. But this was more than that.

Despite the pain that still lit through my lower abdomen, and the adrenaline that pounded through my veins—I could feel it. How everything had changed.

His scent resonated through me. Hanging thick over every inch of my mind, as if his presence drilled a hole straight through my chest directly into the deepest depths of my heart and soul.

The way that his eyes widened, and his jaw dropped open—Mitexi must have realized it too.

But how? This isn't my first time meeting him. How was this happening?

He was more than an attractive bodyguard. More than the guy I'd spent all my free time with. More than just the man who I'd been secretly pining over for weeks now.

Mitexi was my scent match.

ELEVEN

MITEXI

I'd broken down her door to find Pandora sprawled across the floor, half naked. With her teeth gritted and tears streaming down her face as some unknown shit of a man had his teeth to her throat.

I didn't think. I didn't stop. Rage flooded through my veins, as I was on him.

I'd grabbed him right by the jaw, ripping him off her. Pausing just long enough to see that the bite on her neck wasn't complete. He hadn't been casually nipping her or trying to bond her normally—no. I hadn't needed to see her frantic texts minutes before to know the truth. The bite mark was rimmed with darkness. Black tendrils, thin as spider webs, bloomed across the creamy skin of Pandora's neck.

I wanted to kill him.

Anger so white-hot, so consuming I was drowning, it flooded through me. I hadn't quite realized that I'd been pummeling the man, hadn't realized I hit him hard enough to break his bones. Not until I stared at his bloodied face, so mangled he'd need reconstructive surgery before his ugly mug looked fully human again.

Broken and swollen.

All I really wanted was to break him again. Over and over again. For daring to put his hands on *her.*

The soft sound of her gasp cut through the haze of rage. The rage that was stopping me from being able to think. Rage that I was barely holding back. That was whispering sweetly in the back of my ear, how lovely it would be to finish this man off. To make him pay for what he had done to her.

I looked up and met Pandora's eyes, immediately falling under the spell of a completely different threat. The beaten stranger ceased to exist.

I didn't want to admit how often I had pictured what Pandora would look like during her heat.

My fantasies were nothing. Not even the palest shadow compared to reality. They didn't even come *close.*

Pandora was the most gorgeous woman I'd ever seen. The generous curve of her ass. Those full hips that tapered into a tight waist. The sweet curves of perky breasts, the shape of them just visible beneath a thin silky camisole.

Every inch of her was soaked in desire—pheromones and sweat formed a light layer across her skin.

Then, there was her scent.

Pandora had always smelled amazing. Lilies and benzoin. I'd actually gone to a perfume store, on my time off, checking out the different scents to find which one was hers. A smooth and sweet scent like warm vanilla with a hint of spice.

But now?

This wasn't the scent of any omega in heat.

No.

Her scent burned through my lungs, lighting every part of my body on fire.

Her scent was the entire world.

Her scent... was my match.

Mine.

I felt a prickling within my aura, as the edges of my control frayed. After the bonds of my pack shattered, my aura had always run hotter, without the other pack brothers around to stabilize it. I'd thought that going silver status was supposed to help restabilize the trauma of a shattered bond.

But maybe finding out that the beautiful woman I'd been craving, yearning for, was my scent match—right in the middle of her heat. It was too much.

I shivered as I fought myself for control. As heated energy coursed and coiled through my veins.

Hungry and wanting.

If I stayed here any longer, I was going to go right into a rut. It might already be too late to stop it.

Pandora's attacker had used my moment of distraction to hurry out of the room, one hand pressed against his shattered jaw as he stumbled out of the door.

"I need to leave." My voice was strained.

I couldn't let him get away with this. Not after what he'd almost done to her.

I had to track him down and make him pay.

But more importantly... Pandora had been attacked, and had come far too close to being dark bonded. I'd be damned if I ended up being the one to make things worse for her. She deserved far better than that. Better than my fraying control.

Doing right by her was going to fucking destroy me.

Pandora placed her gun down on the floor, her golden eyes locked on mine the entire time. She rose to her feet, making me very aware of the fact that she was half naked.

I tried and failed to look away from her swaying hips, from her dripping center, wet with slick glistening on golden curls, as she walked even closer to me.

I was shaking, holding on to the last dregs of my control. I couldn't just run out on her. I was her bodyguard. I was here to protect her.

Pandora didn't stop until she was standing right in front of me. Tentatively, she reached her palm forward, resting it right on my chest, right over my racing heart.

"Why?" Pandora murmured, as she stroked along my chest lightly.

Just one light touch, and I was hard. Harder than I'd ever been in my entire life.

"Please don't leave me." Her voice was soft, with just the faintest hint of pain in it.

The devastation in her words was so loud she might as well have been screaming.

How could I leave her after what she'd just been through?

How could I trust myself to stay?

I took a deep breath that turned ragged. The air was thick with her. The scent of her desire was all around me. Making my mind heavy. At the same time it felt like all my thoughts were on the verge of floating away. "If I stay in here a second longer, I'm going to fuck you."

Pandora didn't even blink. She watched me, those golden eyes, hooded with lust. Watching me as if I was a puzzle she was trying to figure out.

"What if I want you to fuck me?" Her voice was soft as a purr. So sweet and lovely.

It took a moment for her words to catch up with the fog coating my mind.

She wanted to. She wanted. What?

Oh, fuck *me*.

TWELVE

PANDORA

"Pandora…" Mitexi shook his head slowly. Eyes wide as if I was dense. He spoke fast as if he was forcing the words out before he lost his resolve. "That man just attacked you. He almost… and you're in your heat. I couldn't—"

"Do you want me?" I interrupted him. Careful not to look at the sizable tent in his pants.

"Of course." Mitexi closed his eyes like he was in pain. "But I won't take advantage of you."

I slid my palm down his shirt, feeling along the lines of his chest. Feeling his muscles bunch under my fingertips. "I know what I want."

"You're in heat." He shook his head, never taking his eyes off my body.

"Exactly, and I already talked myself out of calling you half a dozen times during my heat." I took a step closer, breathing in his delicious scent. "And now you're here."

Mitexi shuddered as the last of his control snapped, as he closed the distance between us with a kiss.

It started off sweet. Just the warm press of lips.

Oh, damn.

He felt so *good*. The heat of him. The soft texture of plush lips. The rough calluses on his fingertips that slid against my neck, weaving into my hair, leaving a trail of fire behind in their wake.

I gasped, and he deepened the kiss. Cradling my head in his big hands. I'd never felt so cherished. Been handled so carefully. I was still clutching his shirt by his chest, feeling how his heart pounded for me.

He tasted like everything I ever wanted. A crisp burst of caffeine, with a trace of peppermint. Underneath it all, something spicier, something masculine that tasted undefinable. Something that was just *him*.

I could feel the way that his tongue moved against mine, echoed deep in my core, as I ached for him.

Mitexi broke off the kiss, scooping me off my feet. His breathing was heavier now. Rugged. As he walked with me, placing me back on my heat bed.

He pulled my thin shirt over my head, and his eyes darkened as he took all of me in. Gaze lingering on my breasts, and traveling down my flat belly. Mitexi followed his heated gaze with soft kisses that trailed down my stomach, and along the inside of my thighs. Kissing along them, to the center. He paused there, inhaling deeply like he couldn't get enough.

My breaths became heavier, until I was panting with need. My legs were shivering with anticipation.

What is he going to...

Mitexi swept his tongue right up my slit. All at once, he'd managed to soothe the ache between my legs, and ramp the heat way up. The friction was perfect—pressing in with just the right gentle pressure, circling around my clit, diving deep into me with his tongue.

Fuck.

I had no idea that this could feel so *good*.

Fisting the sheets, I tossed my head back. Drowning in pleasure.

I moaned as the sensations took over, ripping pleasure out of me with a cry that was nothing like me. High pitched and desperate.

"That's it. That's my girl. I want to hear you," Mitexi murmured, with a voice so dark and so deep that it sent shivers down the length of my spine, before continuing his onslaught.

Wracking my core with pleasure, he was feasting on me like he was starving. Consuming me. His tongue sliding and pressing. That soft and persistent suction of his lips. As his grip tightened around my thigh, sliding his other hand up and brushing along my sides to caress the curves of my breasts. Palming them. Rolling my nipples in his fingers and tugging them gently. The added friction ratcheted the tension within me way up.

Until my entire existence boiled down into a bundle of nerves at my core. Throbbing for him so hard I could barely stand it. I grasped the silky locks of his hair, gripping tight. Pushing him against me until the bristle from his five o'clock shadow scraped into my inner thigh.

I pressed him tight against my body, as the bliss within me churned higher and higher. It all broke free as I came. Waves of white-hot bliss rocked me, rolling out from my core to every inch of my body. Leaving me shaking with the aftershocks, and moaning helplessly.

Mitexi licked me gently through my orgasm. Looking up at me smugly like the cat who got the cream, as I lay panting. Recovering, as the last tremors of pleasure shot through me. He crawled over my body, settling himself on top of me. Meeting my lips with another kiss. Delving into my mouth, like he'd just done to my pussy, so I could taste myself on him.

Mitexi settled himself in between my legs as he kissed me. I could feel all of his long length, hard against my thigh. He must have taken off his clothes at some point, while I'd been too distracted to notice.

God, that was going to feel so much better than a vibrator.

Mitexi was right on the same page as me. Reaching down to position himself better.

The moment that I felt his hard dick at my entrance, I froze. Going still as fear pounded through my veins. I felt like I was choking. Like I was drowning. Like all the air in the room was tightening, and I couldn't breathe. As panic swirled around me, all I could focus on was Mitexi's expression.

Mitexi froze with a look of horror on his face, before ripping himself off me.

THIRTEEN
PANDORA

Mitexi lay panting, like he had been sprinting with the devil at his heels. He ran his hands over his face, wiping down hard. It looked like he was fighting himself. Fighting to take control.

Was he going to leave? What if he never wanted to see me again?

Why did I have to go and screw everything up?

I lay completely still. No longer feeling like I was trapped beneath the ice. I'd been able to focus on my breaths. Been able to ward off the panic that had threatened to consume me. Claw across my mind and rip control out from under me.

My breaths shuddered as I tried to force the well of sadness back.

Don't start crying. Don't do it.

Mitexi was still on the bed with me, but he'd put space between us. It was only a foot or two; a distance that felt insurmountable.

Why did I have to react like that? I wanted this. Wanted him. I was still aching for him.

This was exactly the reason why I'd never invited him over during my heat, even though every inch of my body had been craving him. Somehow, I had known that I was just going to fuck this up.

"God, I'm so sorry." Mitexi was gazing at me with wide eyes. His face was pale. Which wasn't fair. He hadn't done anything wrong. "Is this your first time?"

I clenched my eyes shut. Cursing the tears welling up in the corner of my eyes. Hot. Pooling beneath my eyelids and threatening to escape.

"No. It's not." I couldn't look at him, when I admitted it. As soon as I got the words out, he was going to know. Even though I might still look pretty and lovely on the outside, in truth I was none of that. I was broken. "But it's the first time... when I've wanted it."

It was as if the temperature in the room dropped by twenty degrees. As everything went still, my words turned it all to ice.

Mitexi sat upright on the bed, his hand was clenched hard enough that his knuckles turned white. Every one of his veins were bulging, I could practically see the anger coursing through his blood.

I draped my arm over my face, not wanting Mitexi to see me cry. If I pressed hard enough against the tears, maybe I could hold them in. Force them back into the well of pain that I'd become. I held myself tight, struggling not to let out a ragged breath. Not a single stray sniffle. I wouldn't let him know how much his rejection had gotten to me.

"I understand." My voice came out mostly normal, only a little bit strained. "It's okay if you want to go."

I'd ruined everything.

Even before I knew that he was my scent match, he was all I could think about. I wanted him. Wanted him touching me. Wanted him to see all of me. Wanted him in my body, claiming me. I wanted him to be mine.

But I knew better. I knew that if I let him see me—the real me

—that it could break apart everything I'd worked so hard to build back up.

He'd been the only alpha who hadn't terrified me in years.

Without him, how could I trust another bodyguard? Would I be resolved to being trapped in my house for the rest of my life? What if I never found another alpha who I could stand to have around me? Would I be alone for the rest of my life?

I couldn't afford to open myself up to him, but I'd done it anyway. Now what the hell was I going to do?

It was fine.

I'd already resolved to being alone for all the rest of my life. Never expected I could get into a relationship. I was well aware of the fact that I couldn't be with anyone. Not when I was broken.

Then, strong hands gently pried my arm away from my face. Smoothing away the trails of wet streaks that had fallen down both of my cheeks.

Caressing me. Soothing away my pain.

"Hey. This isn't your fault." His voice was deep and kind, even if the words were all wrong.

I shook my head. He didn't—

"I'm not mad at you." Mitexi's light gray eyes were stormy, fixed on me like an avenging God, as he stroked along my cheek. "But I do want to find whoever hurt you and tear them to pieces."

His eyes were filled with an unspoken promise that loosened something with me. Untying a tension that I hadn't even known was there.

I nodded.

The small motion wasn't quite enough to match the fire smoldering in his expression—but it was all I could do to acknowledge that rage on my behalf.

No one had ever gotten so angry for me. Even my parents; they'd hired private detectives of course, and offered a reward for information that would lead to the capture of my kidnappers. But I'd only ever seen relief that I was back.

Mitexi glimpsed behind my pretty exterior, at a hint of the mess that I was underneath. Seen all the ugly truth, and somehow, he hadn't been scared away.

FOURTEEN

PANDORA

An ache built again in my lower belly, too strong to ignore. I couldn't help but give a wistful smile to Mitexi, as I took in the delicious view of his muscular form. Every inch of him looked strong. He looked like he could cut through any danger and keep me safe.

"I've killed-d the mood." I rubbed my cheek, brushing away the last residue of tears there ruefully.

Mitexi just shrugged in reply. As if to wordlessly say *hey, it happens.*

"But we were so close. Things were going perfectly before..." I flushed, the heat in my cheeks burned across me. Stopping me from repeating how I'd embarrassed myself.

"Who said that sex had to be perfect?" Mitexi raised an eyebrow at me.

My mouth snapped shut as I considered his words.

Had anyone said it had to be perfect? Did it have to be?

"So, you still want me?" I winced at how needy and small my voice came out. I wasn't helping my own case at all.

"I don't think that there's anything you could do that would make me stop wanting you." Mitexi's gaze was burning, heating every inch of my body. "If we need to wait, or stop, or take things slow, any of that would be right. I don't care if it's messy. Sex is going to feel perfect, as long as it's with you."

My cheeks were flushed hot, I ducked my head from the intensity of his gaze, taking a steadying breath. "Then I want to start over."

Mitexi cleared his throat, and shifted as if he was suddenly uncomfortable. "You mean, like we never knew each other at all? Start back as friends?"

I shook my head rapidly. *God no.* That was the last thing that I wanted. But I refused to mess this up a second time.

No.

I wasn't going to let my past get the best of me. Not again. I wasn't going to let them win. I knew exactly what I wanted. He was right here. "I want to start today over. Starting with when I told you that I wanted you."

Mitexi frowned as the meaning of my words hit him. "But you just were—"

"Yes, I know." I didn't want to repeat what had almost just happened to me. Didn't want to think about all of the reasons why this probably wasn't a good idea. My therapist would likely have a conniption and have to use those deep breathing and mindfulness techniques on herself if she got wind of what I was planning.

None of that mattered. I didn't care if the timing was wrong or if I was making a mistake. If it was, it was mine to make.

I looked Mitexi right in the eye, at his pupils that had darkened, blown wide with desire. At all the barely restrained passion and desire he had for me. I let the feel of that heat sink into me, soaking me, until I was drowning in want. "I didn't have a choice before. Let me choose you." I leaned in closer, until there was barely the distance of a breath between us. "I want you to remove every trace of them from my skin."

Mitexi's expression was dazed, his eyes half lidded with lust, as he closed the distance between us with a kiss.

His kisses were sweet, as his lips slanted over mine. Taking control, with delicious pressure. He deepened the kiss, and our tongues caressed one another, in a gentle rhythm.

Breaking away to mutter between kisses, "We can stop whenever you want. Just tell me what you need." Before pressing his lips against mine once more, possessively. Claiming me with every soft movement.

He was perfect. Wonderful.

But I wanted more.

I whined, shifting closer to him. I grabbed his hand that was respectfully brushing against my shoulder, pulling it to the curve of my breasts.

"That's it, baby. You're in control. Take exactly what you need." Mitexi growled, as he kneaded me. Right there. Right on my aching nipples, where I needed it.

I was drowning in pheromones. Half drugged by my desire for him. By the delicious scent of his cardamom. He was so fucking delicious. I had to taste him. I licked a strip along his bare chest, tasting the salty masculine essence of him, the sweet spice of baked apple.

"Fuck," he groaned, the word strained as if ripped out of him. He pressed his hot lips to my skin murmuring, "perfect," and "mine," between open-mouthed kisses.

The thrumming in my core pulsed sharper, ripping a high-pitched moan out of me. "Please."

Mitexi hummed, in a deep vibration that heated through me. "Tell me what you need."

I licked my lips, less embarrassed that he was making me say it out loud than relieved that he wasn't going to deny me.

I'd done a fine job of denying myself for far too long.

"I need you to touch me."

Mitexi brushed his calloused finger-tips in feather light brushes against my belly. Igniting every part of me, until I was burning for him. Desperately.

"Baby girl, I'm going to need you to be more specific. You're going to need to tell me *exactly* what you need." Mitexi ran his fingers in a light caress down my side in a pattern that should have been soothing, but was doing nothing but lighting up every one of my nerves. Until I was on fire, and ready to combust.

"Touch my pussy." I forced myself to get the words out, I couldn't take much more of this teasing.

I needed this. Needed him.

Mitexi's fingers trailed down, to exactly the place I needed him. Tracing a path between my folds, until he was caressing my clit. Exerting pressure in a light circular pattern, that was almost perfect.

"More." I begged helplessly. Needing more pressure, more intensity.

Begging helplessly, for that something. That extra bit of pressure and friction. That extra hit of pleasure that would be enough to pull me under.

Mitexi seemed to understand, to take pity on my whimpers that were becoming more and more nonsensical. He lowered his fingers to my entrance, his cool gray eyes locked on mine, as he checked in with me.

I bit my lip, hesitating.

More than anything I wanted him. But I didn't want a repeat of last time, pushing myself beyond what I was ready to handle.

He was so careful with me. So patient. Always making sure never to push beyond my boundaries.

All at once the realization settled over me, warming me from the pit of my stomach—I was safe with him. I could trust Mitexi, he wouldn't ever hurt me.

Taking in a deep breath, I nodded. Signaling for him to keep going.

Slowly, checking my expression the entire time, he pressed a finger into me.

"Tell me how that feels," he murmured.

"Yes," I moaned sharply at the friction. The warm press of his touch within me, the slight stretch as he crooked his finger, moving slowly. The slow, circular pressure of his thumb against my clit. "So good."

This was so much better than a vibrator.

Though I wanted to squeeze my eyes shut and focus on the pleasure, I kept them open. Watching Mitexi the whole time. Reminding myself exactly who was giving me pleasure.

Reminding myself that I was safe, and free to feel *good*.

Until all that tension hit a peak as I came. Pleasure rolled through me, wave after wave of it. Drowning my last lingering worries. Drowning it all in bliss.

As I lay panting, catching my breath, Mitexi kissed me sweetly. Meeting my gaze with understanding in his eyes. "Do you want me to stop?"

I gathered myself together enough to smile at him, relaxed down to my bones.

"I don't think I ever want you to stop."

FIFTEEN
PANDORA

Mitexi had just given me the two most intense orgasms of my life. Now he was watching me catch my breath, like he was ready and waiting to drown me in pleasure once more.

He'd never pushed me, but it didn't matter.

I wanted to push me.

It was more than just the heat pheromones barely held back by my blockers. For the first time in my life I knew what I wanted, and he was right within reach.

I wanted more. I wanted *everything*.

"Mitexi," His name on my lips was a moan. A prayer and a benediction all in one.

His gaze snapped to mine, as his eyes darkened to the color of coal. Smoldering and ready to burn. Just waiting for the signal to ignite.

Every inch of his body was pure strength and feral need. Powerful.

My scent match.

"Fuck me."

His eyes were hooded, dark with desire. More than anything

he stared at me like I was delicious. A whole goddamn meal. While Mitexi looked like a man starving.

But rather than letting things heat up between the two of us, Mitexi scrutinized me. Holding himself back. "You don't have to feel like you have to do anything for me. I can wait."

He was so close.

I took in his sharp jawline. The dark waves of hair that I wanted to run my fingers through. To the hard lines of muscle running down his chest, all the way down to his very hard, very erect cock.

He was perfect. He was safe.

I want him to be mine.

I licked my lips.

His dark gaze zeroed in, tracing every movement of my tongue.

"I don't want to wait." I slid my hands over his shoulders, tracing along the firm lines of muscles. Tugging him towards me.

Mitexi followed me down, closing the distance between us with a hot kiss. Slipping his tongue deep. Tasting me. Cherishing me. Caressing my tongue with his, until that low ache within my lower belly sharpened. Needing him.

His hands were everywhere. Tracing featherlight patterns across my body that were driving me crazy. Mitexi's nostrils flared as he breathed me in. If I smelled to him anything like the way he smelled to me, I couldn't blame him. He was absolutely delicious.

He clenched his eyes shut, his whole body shuddering, and for a moment I was afraid that he was going to turn me down.

"Tell me if it gets to be too much." His voice was so deep I could feel the words sink into me.

I nodded.

It wasn't going to be too much this time.

This was completely different.

I chose this.

"Hey, I mean it. If we need to stop, then we need to stop. We can try again later."

In response I held his gaze, as I slowly spread my legs wide. Watching his pupils dilate, as he noticed how absolutely drenched I was for him.

He settled his torso between my open thighs. Watching me carefully, as he pressed his thick cock against my pussy.

I was ready.

Nodding, I silently signaled for him to keep going.

Mitexi slotted the blunt edge of his cock against my entrance, pressing between the slippery folds of my pussy lips. Then carefully he began to push into me, going so slow that I could feel the slide of every inch of his hard length. I gasped at the *feel* of him. At the perfect pressure of his hardness, right where I needed it. He grabbed my hip tight, steadying me as he kept pressing deeper. Until finally his hips pressed flush against mine as I took him completely.

I tipped back my head, and moaned.

It was all just so *good*.

Lost in the fullness. Perfectly stretched, as the throbbing ache within me was filled with his rock hard girth.

Pleasure overcame everything.

I'd never been so dominated—utterly flooded by raw and intense bliss.

"How does it feel, baby?" Mitexi murmured.

He held himself within me, letting me get used to the size of him. His heated gaze watching my face, checking to make sure that I was alright.

"So good," my words were only half comprehensible. High pitched, and whiny, they sounded more than anything than a plea for more. I grasped Mitexi's back, nails digging in. Overcome by the feel, the heat of it, the warmth of his skin and just needing something to hold on to.

Mitexi pressed heated kisses down my neck. It was crazy how good his kisses made me feel, considering how his dick was currently inside of me.

"Remember baby," he said in between kisses. "You need to tell me how you want it."

"I-I need you to move."

With another light kiss against my neck, Mitexi pulled himself almost all the way out. As he pressed back into me, his cock dragged in a slow slide that seemed to go on forever. Slow enough to let me feel all of him, to memorize the exact shape of him, pressed so close. Reshaping me into someone new—a version of me who wasn't afraid of pleasure.

Which was perfect, because Mitexi was poised to give it to me.

He started moving in a primal rhythm. Rocking gently into me. Those stormy gray eyes, half-hooded with desire, were on mine the entire time. His hips pressed into mine, again and again, in a sensual motion, as Mitexi steadily but insistently claimed me.

He was so fucking big.

Each delicious thrust filled every bit of my aching center— after being numbed and neglected for so long.

I canted my hips, taking him deeper inside of me. Pressing upwards, meeting his strong strokes. Needing this. Needing more of him.

Mitexi growled into my ear, "That's my girl. You take me so well."

Holding himself inside me, he rotated his hips in circular movements that were driving me crazy. I grasped his hand, gripping so hard that my knuckles went white, needing something to hold on to. Letting his sturdy grip steady me, as all the pleasure tugged at me, making me feel like I was coming apart.

I gasped, forcing myself to breathe, taking in his delicious scent with each inhale. Spicy cardamom, with notes that were crisp and sweet. Earthy and masculine. It seemed like he was everywhere. Inside me. His scent was hanging in the air all around me.

So close. All around me. He was everywhere.

He's safe.

I wrapped my legs around Mitexi's waist, arching my back to pull him in closer. This was Mitexi. He'd never hurt me.

Mitexi groaned in his deep voice. The change in the angle made every thrust feel so much more intense. I felt him inside me deeper now.

He leaned against my neck, kissing me hard. Sucking with just the slightest press of teeth—with a desperate edge that I could feel in my blood. Awakening the omega within me who had long been asleep.

Yes. Bite me. Make me yours.

I tried to push down my omega instincts, but she didn't want to be ignored. I squirmed, leaning closer against his harsh kiss. Ripping another high-pitched moan out of me.

I shuddered. It wasn't enough. I wanted him closer. Needed him to take me harder.

I turned to whisper into his ear. "More."

He responded instantly, as if he'd just been waiting for me to give him permission. Slamming himself inside of me.

Hard.

He froze, lines creasing in-between his eyebrows, as his worried gaze snapped to mine.

But it was exactly what I wanted. Everything I'd been denied for so long, it felt he'd broken all of it down. All my loneliness and aching need. All of it replaced by raw strength and pleasure.

"Yes," I squeezed his hand where it intertwined with mine. "Just like that."

He leaned down and pressed his lips against mine in a scorching kiss, before he laid his forehead against mine and began to *move*.

Stormy eyes were locked on mine, as if I was the most precious thing in the world.

His hard cock dove into me, over and over. The hard strokes rocking my entire body. Mitexi was so fucking strong. It was like I was being fucked by a force of nature. By raw and unfiltered strength.

His hips slammed into mine, urgently. Faster. His balls slapped against my ass with each brutal thrust, as his knot thickened at the base of his cock.

As he took me, the pleasure began to rise. Crystalizing into something more.

Mitexi reached down with his free hand, caressing my clit. Pressing down in just the right circular pattern, creating the perfect friction.

I whimpered as the tension rose, squirming against it.

"It's okay baby, I got you." He murmured.

I opened my mouth to protest. All of this was so much. How was I going to be able to handle it?

But something in his steady expression stopped me. Somehow I could feel it. Like I could feel the pounding of my own heart in my chest. That I was going to be alright.

The persistent pressure against my clit, the friction of his cock slamming into me—all of it abruptly shattered as I came. Pleasure, white-hot and molten, erupted all the way down the length of my spine. Rolling through every inch of me, to the far reaches of my body, settling heavy in my limbs.

I shuddered with the aftershocks and Mitexi didn't let up, fucking me through it.

When my climax was over, Mitexi picked up the pace, chasing after his own pleasure. Speeding up and sinking into me, again and again. Grabbing my hips, hard, in a grip that was sure to leave a mark.

With one last powerful thrust, he came. His hips jerked

against mine, as he pulsed deep within me, flooding me with his cum, as his knot swelled. Locking me into place.

His mouth found mine, capturing my lips in a fierce kiss. Pouring into it all the hot desire that my lonely little omega heart had been longing for.

When he broke away panting, Mitexi asked, "Are you alright?"

Within me, his fat knot throbbed as another wave of cum flooded into my core.

A month ago, the thought of an alpha's cock would make me break out into hives. Now I was stuffed full of alpha, and the only reaction I could muster up was a sleepy smile.

"I'm better than I've ever been."

SIXTEEN

MITEXI

Pandora was well on her way to dozing. I stroked my hand through her silky hair, as bright and fine as strands of spun gold.

A knock at the door roused Pandora out of her stupor.

"What was that?" Pandora's voice was wispy. Almost disoriented.

She sounded sated, and thoroughly fucked.

Whether from making love, or the delirium of heat, it didn't matter. A surge of pride came over me. The fact that she looked blissed out, and completely relaxed... I did that. I'd made her feel good.

I kissed her on her temple, whispering, "Don't worry, I'll take care of it."

She settled back down, and her breathing evened out. After over a dozen rounds, she'd finally fallen asleep. Her heat was slowing down, and would likely break completely while she rested.

I don't even know how many hours it had been. Probably longer than a day, and I didn't have anything with me. I wasn't about to go answer her bedroom door naked. My clothes were filthy with sweat, and traces of her attacker's blood, but I had to put them on, since I had no others. After getting dressed, I sniffed myself, before opening the door. Maybe it would be a good idea for me to stop by my house and take a shower before Pandora got up.

I stepped outside, as quietly as I could, not wanting whoever it was to wake Pandora. I'd done a number on the door, hacking off the knob with a fire extinguisher. The metal part of it was still attached, hanging on by a wish and a prayer. The door still shut, just not very well.

Outside Pandora's heat room was an entire squadron of alphas from the police force.

I'd worked with a couple of them in the past. The officers were sometimes the first responders on a scene. They'd work with me to secure the scene, as my pack did our part with extricating victims from crashes, or putting out fires.

"What can I do to help you, Officer Thompson?" I said, using my professional first-responder voice for the first time in months.

Thompson shifted a bit, as if he was uncomfortable. "I'm sorry about this Mitexi, but I'm here to arrest you."

What? Arrested?

There had to be some kind of mistake.

"What am I being arrested for?" I looked around at all their solemn faces. Half expecting for some of them to start to break out into smiles. To tell me that they were just kidding and let me know what was really going on.

But of course, none of them moved.

"For the attempted murder of Daniel Hinman."

I was floored, and feeling incredibly stupid. Standing here at my own arrest, in a shirt partly splattered in my victim's blood.

"You have the right to remain silent. Anything you say can and will be used against you in the court of law."

Great, I was getting arrested for attacking the man, and I hadn't even made it worthwhile. I should have killed him when I had the chance. Obviously, I couldn't leave Pandora vulnerable during her heat, but I should have made those first handful of blows count.

One of the officers I didn't recognize, fresh faced and eager-looking, pulled out the handcuffs from his utility belt.

"That isn't necessary." Officer Thompson stated, giving the rookie a hard look until the man put his cuffs away. "Mitexi is going to come along quietly."

I nodded dumbly. following the officers out of the Delano house. Unsure if I was ever going to be allowed to return and see my mate again.

SEVENTEEN
MITEXI

The officers put me in my own holding cell. I guess it was their way of separating me from the other criminals. Maybe they were trying to let me know that they didn't think of me in the same way as they did the other people they'd arrested. Perhaps that I didn't deserve to be here.

Not that it mattered. I was incarcerated, same as anyone else.

God, I had a record now. What would my father say if he was alive to see this? What the hell had happened to my life?

The isolation was getting to me, even at home I had Fireball to keep me busy. I'd counted all the painted cement blocks making up the side of the cell. Counted all of the dead spiders in the dusty upswept corners. Memorized the exact contour of the smudge at the bottom edge of the cell. Until the hours blurred together into something unrecognizable.

Quick footsteps and the jangle of keys had me jumping up to my feet. Officer Thompson was unlocking my cell, and opening the door wide. "You've been bailed out."

I got to my feet, brushing off imaginary dust, trying to think of who would have bailed me out, and coming up blank. My parents were gone. My pack was gone. I'd neglected friendships for years. Though I had some distant cousins, they didn't know that I'd been taken into custody. Even if they had known, they didn't have the kind of money to get me out of here.

Even if I had someone to call, I had priorities. I'd used my one phone call to ask my neighbor to check in on Fireball.

I followed Officer Thompson to a receiving area, and my eyes locked straight on to a formidable woman. Silk blouse and a crisp blazer over the shoulder. Delicate thin strapped sandals under perfectly tailored pants, and a handbag that probably cost more than I made in half a year. Her platinum blonde hair was cut in a sleek bob. More than any one feature, or expensive article of clothing or accessory, she had that indefinable air of wealth that hung about her—clinging to every one of her polite and poised expressions like a second skin. This was Mrs. Delano, Pandora's mother.

Besides the interview process, and my first day of employment, I hadn't had much interaction with Mrs. Delano.

Ice blue eyes scrutinized me, taking in my sweat and blood-stained apparel. I knew that I must smell like the worst combination of days of sex and stale confinement.

I couldn't break the silence. What did I possibly say to her?

Mrs. Delano had charged me with keeping her daughter safe, and instead I'd slept with her. After that, what could she want with me? I wasn't looking forward to finding out exactly what she had to say to me.

"Mr. Lee, I apologize for all this inconvenience." She spoke in her polished tone, though the words were all wrong. She was discussing this as if I had to wait too long at the doctor's office, which was grossly sugar coating the truth; I'd been arrested. For nearly killing a man. Though I'd unapologetically believed that I hadn't quite tried hard enough to do the job right.

Maybe for that thought alone, I deserved to be back in that cell.

"Would it be possible for you to come along with me? There's a matter I'd like to discuss with you."

I nodded, still numb.

Was she firing me then? Couldn't she just do that over a phone call or something? There was no point in having a whole meeting about it.

I followed Mrs. Delano into her company car, where she ignored me, scrolling through her phone, tapping out emails and messages for the entire ride. Bringing me straight from the county station back to the Delano family mansion, where I'd been detained.

She didn't speak to me until we were back in her office. With her sandalwood desk, and fountain pen between the two of us, Mrs. Delano sat in her sleek office chair and finally spoke to me.

"Sorry about the delay, I'd only recently been informed about the situation." Mrs. Delano shuffled some paperwork on her desk, arranging the corners so that they lined up perfectly. She grabbed a pencil, hand poised and ready for note-taking, before fixing me with her ice blue gaze. "Tell me exactly what happened."

I sighed deeply, running my fingers through my hair. Mrs. Delano wanted more details about how I'd fucked her daughter?

I was definitely getting fired for this.

"Pandora sent me a text message. She sounded panicked."

"Can you tell me the content of the text message?" Mrs. Delano frowned at her paper.

"She'd heard a noise, and thought that someone was trying to break into her heat room."

"I see. Was that a ruse of some sort? Was she trying to get you into the room?"

"No ma'am. It wasn't a ruse. When I came into her room, I saw an alpha holding her down and trying to dark bond her."

Mrs. Delano's pencil snapped sharply against the page. She held up the broken edge close to her face, examining it. With a sigh, she placed the pencil down flat at her desk, pushing her notes away entirely. "That wasn't what I was told."

I shrugged, not knowing what to say to that. It was the truth.

"So that's why you…" Her voice trailed out.

"I broke Daniel's jaw." My voice lowered as anger flooded through me. He deserved so much worse for what he'd done. "I wanted to kill him."

"While I understand the sentiment, I advise you not to mention that again." Mrs. Delano's lips pinched together, as she shook her head slightly. "Then Mr. Hinman managed to get away?"

"I got distracted…" God, Mrs. Delano wasn't really going to ask for more details. I did *not* want to talk about my sex life with my boss. "We scent matched."

"I see that the version of events I was told wasn't exactly accurate," she said in a low voice. "We might be able to settle with Mr. Hinman, and have your charges dropped. Let the lawyers handle it."

Perhaps I should have felt some sort of relief at her words. Maybe I wasn't going to end up in jail. Instead I was just unsettled. Unrooted. The feeling was uncomfortably familiar. Once again, I was staring in the face of a disaster. Everything in my life was torn apart, and I watched it all crumble, while I was powerless to do anything about it.

"My daughter is your scent match, and she is very fond of you."

I said nothing, sensing that the other shoe was about to drop. The "but" left unspoken. We were finally getting to the point of all this entire meeting. The reason she had bothered to bail me out of jail in the first place. Was she going to fire me? Honestly, I'd been waiting for that since the moment that I'd slept with my protectee.

"I'm prepared to give you two and a half million dollars, for you to offer my daughter a princess bond."

What?

Two and a half million? Dollars?

It wasn't that I'd gotten a poor salary as a first responder, but I wasn't even able to think about money at that scale.

I wiped a hand across my face, trying to hold in the hysterical laughter threatening to escape.

"No."

I never thought that I would be in a position to turn down that type of money.

Mrs. Delano frowned, "I'm prepared to offer as high as three million."

I shook my head, not wanting to hear it.

I had to approach this like a bandaid. Rip it straight off. I couldn't give it a chance to sit and fester in my mind until it began to sound like a good idea to me. "I'm not going to take payment for a princess bond."

No amount of money was going to make me change my mind. Even at ridiculous amounts the Delano family was able to wave at me.

Mrs Delano sighed, putting her pencil carefully back on the table. "This is something that could significantly improve Pandora's quality of life. As you do seem to genuinely care for my daughter. The offer stands. I'll give you time to reconsider."

I nodded, though I already knew it wasn't going to happen.

As I let myself out of the office, I was prepared to see anyone other than Pandora standing there, right outside the door.

Beautiful Pandora. Freshly showered and wearing a gorgeous sundress. She was the definition of angelic, as she stared at me with wide eyes and a devastated look on her delicate features.

My mouth hung open as words and explanations escaped me.

Wait, how much had she heard? It wasn't what it sounded like.

Pandora's full lips quivered slightly, as she spoke in the softest voice I'd ever heard her use.

"You don't want to bond with me?"

EIGHTEEN
MITEXI

I closed the door behind me with a snap, giving us some privacy.

"Hey," I wanted to wrap Pandora in a huge hug, shutting all the world away. Not coming out until I'd made this right. But that would probably make her think the wrong thing, after overhearing that conversation with her mother. I settled for lightly brushing away the small tear that leaked down her cheek. "Can we talk about this?"

She startled, like I had shocked her. She took a deep breath, as if preparing herself for bad news.

I smiled at her, hoping to convey wordlessly that it was going to be alright.

Pandora walked by my side like she was in a daze. Like she was on the verge of breaking down, just holding back tears. I planned on taking that look away from her as soon as possible. I wasn't stupid enough to let a simple miscommunication between us grow out of control, breaking this wonderful thing that we had just started between the two of us.

She was silent for the entire walk back to her room.

I followed her in, softly shutting the door behind us, and firmly latching the deadbolt into place.

Pandora's room looked like something that came straight out of a home design magazine. Everything came in soft creams and lavender, from the wispy curtains to the modern loveseat across from a full-length antique mirror. Her room was all sleek and designer minimalism—from the crown molding to the full-sized crystal chandelier that could easily make the front page, or go viral on social media. All of it was luxury far beyond my pay grade. I should probably be paying some sort of admittance fee to even step into her space.

Though Pandora was living in the kind of wealth I could barely fathom, why was it that she was looking at *me,* like I had all the power at the tip of my fingers? As if I would be the one to break her heart?

Pandora had somehow gotten our relationship all twisted up. Didn't she know that from the first moment I saw her, *she* became my every reason?

Why I woke up in the morning. Why I went through my daily routine with a goddamn smile on my face. Why for the past few months I had stopped feeling like I was just going through the motions of life, just waiting. I don't even know what I was waiting for. For the weekends. For that next chance to just lie in bed, eating chips and watching whatever happened to be on the television. Just powering through, not to disappoint those few people who still relied on me.

I must be doing something wrong if she had no idea that every single breath I took was for her.

How I watched her with a silent prayer on my lips thanking every god, that I had found her.

Pandora spoke. Soft. Delicate and broken.

"Do you not want me?"

My gorgeous girl seemed to be shrinking into herself. Pandora wasn't even meeting my eyes.

Shit.

She actually thought that I didn't want her? That wasn't my intention at all.

What would it even mean that I didn't want to bond her?

Did she think that even though we were scent matched, that I wasn't serious about her? That I just wanted to fuck her, as if this was only some casual thing for me?

Pandora sniffed, blinking rapidly. Her lovely eyes were suddenly red rimmed.

I wasn't going to waste another minute letting her think that she didn't mean anything. When she meant everything.

"Fuck the money. I want you."

My voice was low, the words came out like a growl.

Of course, I fucking wanted her. I always wanted her. I wanted her right goddamn now. I'd happily throw her onto the bed, and fill her once more with my cum. To bite down on her. Hard. Until it broke that creamy skin and I could taste her blood on my tongue. I wanted to leave my mark on her. Let everyone fucking know that she belonged to me.

"What?"

Her gaze snapped to mine, her eyes went completely round as if what I'd said had shocked her.

"I've wanted you since the first moment I saw you. I want you more than anything." I couldn't keep the heat out of my words. But that might have been because I wanted her to feel it. To let that heat sink into her very bones, until she knew without a doubt how I ached for her.

"Then... why don't you want to bond with me?"

So much was taken from her. I refused to let her think that our relationship wasn't solid.

That I wasn't doing this for her.

"I don't want to get paid to bond with you. I didn't want you to think that I was only going to offer you a princess bond because someone was waving their checkbook at me. Taking up that offer, it would be taking the choice away from you."

Pandora swiped away tears on her cheek. "Taking my choice? I don't understand."

"I wasn't going to assume that you even wanted to bond with me, or when and how you'd want to do it. If I took money to bond with you, then what kind of say would you have in it? You should be able to talk about it, do it on your own terms. I know that we've only just gotten together, but my relationship with you is too important to fuck up with money."

Pandora looked up at me through wet lashes. "So... you do want to bond?"

She looked like a sad-eyed angel. Like absolute perfection.

How the fuck had I gotten into the position to have this gorgeous girl asking me about something as intimate as bonding? How had I gotten so fucking lucky?

Except I couldn't just let her choose me. Not unless she knew everything.

"Baby... I just signed up for silver status. You have to know that if you are with me, you will never have a pack. I can't give that to you. You have so many choices."

Pandora laughed, a bitter laugh that sounded nothing like happiness.

"I don't have choices." She shook her head slowly, as if she was willing me to understand. "Before I'd met you, I hadn't left the house in years. I was terrified. Terrified of alphas. Of getting hurt again. The thing is, I let that fear control me. I don't think that you have any idea how much it completely took over my life. Nobody understood it. Not my parents. None of my therapists. They think I've thrown my whole life away. That I was just letting it all go. Giving up."

Pandora stared off into a far corner of her room, staring at nothing. She smiled ruefully—just the faintest tug at the corner of her lips. "I think that my dad is sick of it. He hasn't even spoken to me in two weeks."

"Baby..." I didn't know what to say to her. Didn't know how to make things right. I don't think that there actually was any way to make what had happened right. What was worse, I had no idea what exactly had happened to her. Just the small amount that she'd hinted at was enough to fill me with rage.

I was starting to get the sinking suspicion that what she'd gone through was so much worse than even that small amount she'd hinted.

"Since... then... you're the only one that's ever been safe." Pandora took a step closer to me, placing her warm palm on my chest. The look in her eyes was vulnerable, as she stared up at me through those fine blonde lashes. "I don't want a pack. I just want you. Only you."

My jaw dropped as my breathing quickened. Each breath taking in her sweet scent, that sophisticated mix of lilies and benzoin. That suave fragrance that was like smooth vanilla with a trace of spicy cinnamon. It was in the air all around me, reminding me with each sweet inhale that she was my scent match.

Mine.

I cradled her face, brushing against cheeks that were still damp with tears.

She wanted me?

Just as I was? Silver status and all?

Well, I would never stand in the way of Pandora getting anything that her heart desired. She deserved it all. The whole fucking world.

My lips crashed into hers. Kissing her with all of the fire roaring in my blood.

NINETEEN
MITEXI

I pressed open-mouthed kisses across her neck.

Kissing her hard with a hint of my teeth right against the spot where I was desperate to claim her. To bond her, marking her as mine.

Not yet.

Pandora had only just told me that she wanted me.

But baby, I'm starving for you.

Taking her mouth in a rough kiss, I tasted her sweetness. My tongue brushed against hers. The slide, that lovely friction and heat, it sent every ounce of blood in my body straight to my cock.

When I was already painfully hard.

I backed her up against the wall, pressing against her a little too hard. A little too desperately, and unable to stop myself.

I was completely lost in the feel of her skin, like silk beneath my fingertips. Tracing over each of her curves. Feeling the heat of her breath against the crook of my neck as she gasped.

My fingers bit into her perfect skin a bit too rough. I had to hold myself back, or I'd end up giving her bruises.

I toyed with the hem of her cotton sundress, brushing the tips of my fingers against her luscious thighs. Cupping the soft curve of her ass, and urging her to wrap her legs around me.

My gorgeous girl did so, eagerly. She moaned softly as I ground myself against her hot core.

"Look at what you do to me. You're such a good girl."

In between hot kisses, I praised her. "Perfect girl. I fucking want you." My voice deepened, into a growl. "You're mine."

I grasped Pandora's ass securely. Crossing the room with her. Refusing to let up from my caresses, I fumbled awkwardly with the door to her bathroom. Once inside I jerked the faucet on, carrying Pandora directly under the spray.

She shrieked as the cold water hit her.

"Shit, sorry." I murmured, reaching behind me to adjust the temperature.

As the water warmed, Pandora's light cotton sundress was soaked. Clinging to her chest perfectly. Subtly revealing a hint of her rosy nipples, like a second skin.

I stroked along the curve of her breasts, fully enveloping them, and kneading at the soft flesh.

I leaned my head down, taking a direct hit from the lukewarm spray of the shower. Sucking one of her tits right into my mouth, fabric and all.

Pandora gasped as I suckled at her, arching her back and pressing even closer to my questing lips.

I wanted to devour her. Consume every inch of her tight body.

Pandora's eyes became heavy-lidded and her gasps became higher. Sharper and more desperate. I reached down, running my hands across the smooth skin between her thighs. Her skin was the earth's softest silk. Her sighs were angelic.

She was delicate, and oh so lovely.

She was going to take all of me.

I slipped my fingers beneath the band of her soaking panties, reaching down through sodden curls to the heat between her thighs. I stroked along her pussy, stroking her firmly, in circular patterns. My eyes were glued to her expression the entire time. To the exact pressure that made her voice hitch slightly. The movements that made her mouth drop open, as a sweet moan was dragged out of her.

Then caressing her clit, teasing it with light touches, until Pandora squirmed. Making her moan louder, as her head fell all the way back, resting against the pristine marble tiles.

I flicked against her clit harder, in the slow patterns that drove her crazy, as I sunk one finger into her entrance. I couldn't peel my eyes away from her, as her own eyes clenched shut. A strangled moan, that sounded vaguely like my name was ripped out of her.

Within her, her walls pulsed, contracting in ripples that gripped desperately at my finger, as she came with a shriek.

I carefully pumped my hand, touching her walls and not easing off her clit for one second. Keeping up the pressure, determined to draw her orgasm out for as long as I could.

"That's my good girl. You came so sweetly for me." I murmured to her.

Pandora was a goddess when she came. Unearthly and perfect.

"Can my good girl take all of me?" My eyes were locked on hers.

Silently praying that she was ready for more. My cock was painfully hard, every instinct in my body was begging me to ram myself into her. To bear down on her and take her.

Her eyes shone with need as she came down. "Yes," she moaned. "I need more."

Oh, thank fuck.

Shoving my pants down, my freed cock slapped against my abs, pointing straight at the ceiling. Jerking her panties to one side, I aligned myself with her sweet pussy, pushing myself into molten bliss. My groan was guttural and loud, as I ground myself into her all the way to the hilt. Forcing myself to hold back, to check in on her, instead of pounding into her mindlessly like a beast.

Pandora's head was tipped back with her mouth opened in an 'o' of surprise. Her eyes were clenched shut. Her back flush against the cool marble tiles.

She exhaled, letting out one stuttering breath, before she opened those gorgeous eyes. Pandora looked up at me through long lashes, her expression softened as it met mine. I recognized what that meant. She trusted me.

What had I done to deserve her?

Tightening my grip on her hips, I pulled almost all the way out of her, thrusting back in hard. Watching her eyes—now half lidded with lust, as they closed in pleasure.

Pandora whimpered, arching her back, and stretching her legs open wider. Letting me take her deeper.

Growling my approval, I leaned in closer. Kissing and nipping across her neck. Into the luscious curves of her sweet tits, suckling through the thin fabric that was doing a poor job of keeping her dressed, all as I pounded into her in a slow rhythm. Making sure to grind into her sweet spot, hard enough to make this good for her.

I whispered into the shell of her ear, "That's my girl. You take me so well."

Pressure was building, from a heaviness in my balls, to a pleasure that shivered all the way along my spine. I wasn't going to last.

I was lost to sensation—The shower water cascading down my back. Slippery skin brushing against me. The warmth of her thighs around my hips. Delicious friction running down every inch of my cock. The perfect heat of her pussy all around me. The rhythmic slap of my balls against Pandora's ass. The ripple of her supple flesh as I thrust into her.

I needed her too damn badly. Pressure was churning within me. My balls were tight and throbbing. Everything in me was screaming to release. But not yet.

Adjusting my grip on her, I held her tight in one arm. Reaching down through slick curls to her center. Pressing hard against her pussy, cupping her tight.

"This is mine."

"All yours." Pandora echoed. In a voice that was half lost to delirium. Drowning in pleasure.

Circling pressure right where she needed it. She was tense, right on that edge. Squirming, and needy, and so, so close. I slapped her, right against her clit, growling into the shell of her ear. "Come for me."

She detonated. Moaning. Shaking with the intensity of her orgasm that gripped my cock, as her walls fluttered around me.

At the sight of her arched backwards, her eyes clenched shut in ecstasy, I couldn't hold myself back. With one last sharp thrust, I came. Pulsing deep within her. Feeling the warmth of my cum bursting free and marking her as mine. My knot swelled, at the base of my cock. Pressing me even more firmly against the heat of her. Locking me in, exactly where I wanted to be.

The two of us were drenched. Completely sodden with water and arousal and the cum that slipped out. I slid down to my knees, setting Pandora down with care.

She clung to me, panting. Water dribbled down across us both. I just held her, not wanting to let go. I would be more than happy to lay down and sleep there, on the shower floor, covered in warm steam and wrapped around my girl.

Eventually my knot softened enough that I was able to slip out of her. A rush of cum leaked out, spilling over the tiles on the floor. My milky essence pooled around the drain, slowly getting washed away by the slow shower spray.

All I wanted to do was gather it up and press it back into my girl. Until my mark was on her neck, for everyone to see, I just wanted my claim inside of her, where it belonged. But that was irrational. I *knew* that my thoughts weren't making sense. My semen inside of her didn't make Pandora any more mine. That was all up to *her.* And my girl had already made her decision.

Beneath me, Pandora squirmed, and I shifted my weight off her. She narrowed her eyes at my pants that had ended up wrapped around my ankles as if they personally offended her, plucking at the soaked fabric.

"You didn't take off your pants," with a quick glance down she added, "or socks."

I shrugged. "I couldn't wait to get inside of you."

Pandora shook her head. "Next time I'm getting you completely naked."

Next time?

My cock twitched with interest.

Gripping her under her knees and at her back, I lifted her. Striding out of the bathroom and headed to the pristine lavender sheets of her bed, as my cock began to stir to once more.

"Well then, baby girl, let's make that happen."

TWENTY
MITEXI

As the post-coital haze began to wear off, I could tell that there was something wrong. As I kissed along Pandora's shoulders, stroking soothing patterns along her back, I could feel it. My girl was tense.

I kissed her temple, "What's wrong?"

Pandora tensed up, hunching her shoulders tight.

I stroked a soothing pattern along her back, "You can tell me."

Pandora didn't say a word, holding herself perfectly still.

If she wasn't ready to talk about it, that was fine. I opened my mouth to say that I was here to listen, whenever she was ready, when Pandora broke the silence.

"I-I haven't been able to sleep. I keep picturing someone breaking in. Then I try to tell myself that it's safe and it's all in my head, but saying the words doesn't change anything."

Pandora's hands began to shake. I took her hand in mine, squeezing it, letting her know that I was here for her.

I hadn't even anticipated how triggering the attack could be on Pandora emotionally. It was too close of a repeat of what had happened to her so many years before.

How violating would that feel? For a stranger to break into her very home. The one place that was supposed to be safe? No wonder she was having trouble getting to sleep.

"Stay with me." The words were out of my mouth, making my offer before I could think better of it. Here, Pandora had the best security system money could buy. She had her luxurious linen, designer furniture, and attack dogs.

The only protection I had to offer was well. Me.

This had been her only home for so many years. I didn't mean to feel like I was intruding. I wasn't trying to make her choose between me and her safe space.

"You'd be okay with that?" She looked up at me through her lashes. Her eyes, watery and hopeful.

"I wouldn't have offered, if I wasn't."

She sniffed, nodding. I could feel the motion of it against my chest.

For one brief moment, a feeling of alarm bubbled up—I brushed it to the side, ruthlessly. I don't know what it was. Something was vaguely worrying me, but it didn't matter. Nothing was more important than keeping her safe.

Some minutes later, I helped Pandora pack. By helping, I was mainly just standing holding her bag in a walk-in closet big enough to be its own room.

"The cerulean or the cobalt?" She held up two hangers with blue dresses. One slightly darker than the other.

Pandora was staring at me expectantly.

"They're both nice," I nodded, eyeing the slinky fabric. She'd look hot in either dress. Honestly, Pandora could wear a pillowcase and make it look designer. Not that I was going to tell her that.

She stared at me, with a deadpan expression.

Okay, not what she was looking for.

I pointed to the darker dress. "That one."

The lighter dress had cut-outs that were hot as all hell, but a lower neck-line. I didn't want anyone to be around the delicate creamy skin of her neck. Not until the two of us were bonded, and the threat of a dark bond was off the table.

She nodded thoughtfully, folding the dress I picked into the traveling bag, and hanging the other back up.

After she'd piled what seemed like a quarter of her wardrobe into her suitcase, before grabbing another bag and neatly placing purses inside.

When she was done filling her bag of designer bags, she wrung her fingers nervously.

"I need to send a text message to my mother."

Pandora tapped out a message, then paused, her finger hovering over the send button. "I feel like this is something that I should be saying to her in person."

"Do you want to stop by her office?"

She shook her head. "I don't want to see the look on her face. I won't be able to handle it if she asks me to stay. I'm going to start crying." Pandora tapped the send button decisively, dropping her phone unceremoniously into her purse. "I'm done crying."

I followed Pandora out to her driver, treating the entire affair as if I was still her bodyguard. Though the entire house felt colder, emptier, now that Pandora would shortly no longer be a part of it.

This mansion, the salary, none of it mattered as much as making sure that Pandora was safe. I was going to be exactly where I needed to be—wherever my girl needed me.

I'd keep her away from any asshole who would dare to hurt her.

Unlocking the door of the apartment for my omega was not the ideal time to remember that I'd left the laundry half done. I could only hope that instead of half-assing it and dumping clothes on the bed, I'd quarter-assed it and left them out of sight in the dryer.

As soon as I opened the door, Fireball ran up to me, yowling his little head off, as if he couldn't spend more than a second in my scent match's presence without letting her know that he was the most spoiled cat in the universe.

"Hey, Fireball," my voice changed as if I was talking to a baby as I scooped up the little miscreant. Fireball permitted me to cuddle him for almost twenty seconds, before he wiggled out of my hand, charging off into the house, in the direction of his foodbowl.

He turned back to check to see if I was following, and meowed the saddest meow—letting the world know that he was starving, surely on the verge of perishing. All of that was ridiculous. My neighbor had texted that he'd left the little liar a full bowl of his favorite food just a few hours ago. I followed him anyway, lugging Pandora's things.

"I better go feed this guy," I muttered, glancing at my girl's face. God, what if she thought I was abandoning her in favor of the cat, the moment that she stepped into this place?

But she just smiled.

"He's cute."

I led Pandora into the living room, carefully placing her bag of clothes and her bag of bags down on the sofa, before crossing over to the four tiered cat tower that dominated a full corner of the room. I placed a handful of treats down—yes the vet had told me that Fireball could lose a couple pounds, but we had to make a good impression. There was no way he was going to be anything other than a terror unless his belly was all the way full.

As soon as I had fed the fluffy monster, I swallowed the lump growing in my throat. This was the first time anyone had entered the apartment since... I'd lost them, and their relatives had come to pick over what was left.

"Umm, let me show you around."

There wasn't much to see. I hadn't anticipated finding my

scent match. All plans of preparing for an omega had gotten completely derailed.

If I'd had the slightest idea that Pandora was the one, I would have gone all out. Arranging the furniture, making sure that I left everything just right. I would have spent hours mopping every inch of the floorboards, and gotten all new furniture. Everything that she deserved. I would have started up a new credit card with Nesting Needs and decked out her space with all the best fabrics. If she wanted those sparkly fairy lights, or the hanging plants, anything. She'd get it.

I had thought that those dreams had died along with the old me. No one was more surprised than me to watch them rise from the ashes phoenix-like.

Pandora was here. We still had time.

I opened the door to my own room, revealing the minimal furniture. There was nothing in the space but my bed. At least I'd upgraded to a queen size bed because I'd been paranoid of squishing Fireball after he'd insisted on cuddling with me.

Never before had I realized how gloomy my gray comforter looked. With that damning single pillow. My standard metal bed frame was nothing like the ornately carved wooden bedframe in Pandora's room that looked taken straight out of a fairy tale. I didn't even have any photographs—I'd taken them all down. No plants, not even a stack of books to mark the room as mine. The only thing to distinguish this room from a prison cell was the stack of brightly colored cat treats stacked on my otherwise barren desk.

Pandora stepped through the room, with an inquisitive air. Stepping around slowly as if my room was an exhibit in some museum. She headed back out into the living room, looking at the rest of the house.

Pandora looked at everything with curiosity. No judgment was hidden in the depths of her lovely eyes, though she must be used to the highest quality of everything. Not this generic furniture, all pre-packaged and built for assembly.

"What's behind those other doors?" She casually took a step closer to one.

A stone fell in the pit of my stomach.

It wasn't as if I'd forgotten them. No. I remembered them. Always. Their absence weighed on me constantly. Like a chunk was ripped out of me that constantly throbbed. I just hadn't realized that I would have to show that void within me to someone else.

Wordlessly, I crossed to the first door and opened it.

The room smelled stale. Like dust that had gotten too comfortable. I tried to tell myself that the room still smelled like the bergamot in Tycho's fancy after-shave. The vague scent of his sweat after working out. But after all of these years, even I could admit that it wasn't true.

His room looked like nothing so much as a patch-work graveyard. Knick knacks left untouched behind closed doors. An old coffee mug covered in a fine layer of dust, that I hadn't dared to move since the last moment it had touched Tycho's lips all those years ago.

Some messy paperwork that I hadn't put back. I wouldn't be able to touch it without seeing the stoic look on the face of Tycho's father, as he rifled through his things, grabbing a handful of valuables and leaving all the rest.

Pandora didn't say a word. Her eyes widened slightly, as she walked around the space, not touching a single thing. Not asking any questions.

She stepped out of the room, walked to another of the closed doors, gazing at me in a silent question.

I nodded, and Pandora turned the knob, stepping through the door.

Will's room was nothing but a shell. A week or so after the

funeral, an army of his relatives had come over. All of Will's cousins worked together to haul away most of the furniture and exercise equipment. The lot of them were so organized that I hadn't even realized that they were finished until I passed by the open door, and faced all of Will's missing things, neatly excised, leaving a gaping hole behind as if he had been taken from me all over again.

I don't even remember the exact layout anymore. Where had his bed been? His desk? It bothered me more than it should have that I didn't remember the exact color of his desk. It was like he didn't quite exist anymore. Like if I didn't even have the right memory of him, was he even important to me at all?

All that was left in Will's room were the few things that his family hadn't wanted. There was a mostly empty bottle of his two-in-one shampoo. A filing cabinet that jammed a little, it had to be wiggled just right to open. On top of it was some dusty junk mail, an application for a credit line.

That was all that was left to show that Will was ever even here.

Pandora left, heading for the last unopened door.

I rarely went into Chase's room. Couldn't be in there without picturing his sister, sobbing quietly as she carefully wrapped up his things. She'd taken down the motivational posters that used to hang around the walls. His collection of soda bottles with quirky designs.

Every item that she took away lessened the presence of him.

Maybe if everything was left how it was, I could remember what it felt like having his bubbly optimism flowing through the bond—his stead-fast hopefulness that everything was going to be okay.

All I could do was cling to the scraps that remained.

The slightly wrinkled post-its that clung to his wall, a fine dust layered over the bright neon colors.

His dresser, still stuffed with all of his clothes.

The calendar on his wall, stuck on his last month. Labeled with doctor's appointments and birthdays, with goals scribbled in the margins.

The 32 ounce water bottle that he used to carry around with him everywhere. Now empty and tipped over in the corner of the room.

It took me a few minutes to realize that I was alone. Still staring at the blue tinted plastic of a dusty old water bottle. How long had I spaced out just staring at it?

Shit? Where was she? Had I managed to scare her off, in the first few minutes that I'd shown her my place? Maybe I was too close to myself to notice that I was a walking red flag. As lost as these sad relics, that was all that was left of my pack.

Maybe she was just now realizing that most of who I was had died along with them. That all I had to offer was the jagged and broken bits that remained after the moment that the bond was ripped out of me.

Pandora had quietly gone to sit on the sofa, next to her things. I was only now noticing how scratched up it was along the arm-rest.

I stood silently. Waiting. Like I was at the doctor's office bracing for news. Waiting for the moment that Pandora told me that she had made a mistake and to please take her back home.

Her voice got quiet as she asked, "Can you tell me about them?"

TWENTY-ONE
MITEXI

What was there to say about them?

What do you say about the gaping hole that lives in your chest where your heart is supposed to be? The one that everyone treats like something that should be healed, only it's still raw.

But I couldn't stay silent, saying nothing to Pandora. This was my scent match.

Will. Chase. Tycho...

They were supposed to be hers too.

I pulled out the wallet, reaching behind the once crumpled post-it with Chase's list of affirmations.

I am successful

I am strong.

I am living with abundance.

I am grateful to be alive.

Funny how none of those affirmations felt remotely true for me. Not for all the years I've read them trying to feel something. No. I hadn't even felt alive, forget feeling gratitude for my life. Not until I'd met *her*.

Behind the post-it I'd placed a picture of my pack. It wasn't even taken that long before our last call.

I didn't take it out too often. It hurt too much.

Wordlessly, I handed the picture to Pandora.

She was supposed to have more than a picture of them. She was meant to have all of their love. All of Chase's enthusiasm, and Will's determination. That fiery passion brimming in Tycho that he'd hid just under the surface.

Will. Chase. Tycho. They were all good men.

Pandora had lost them all. She'd never even get to know what she'd lost. Never even got a chance to meet them.

I cleared my throat. Had to say something about them.

"The tall one is Will. He's standing next to Chase, the blonde guy with the navy blue hoodie. Those two were the fastest sprinters on a firesquad for a hundred miles. Between them, they'd saved the lives of two dozen people, five or six dogs and a parrot. Will was a brave man. Dedicated and hardworking. While Chase, he was an idealist. The type to always see the best in everybody. The two of them were always pushing one another far and beyond what anyone thought was possible."

"Will and Chase," Pandora murmured. Her gaze flicked to mine in the photo, and the man I'd had my arm around.

It felt like my throat was closing up thinking about Tycho. Sharing about him after he'd been gone so long. He was so much more than an old and faded picture hidden in someone's wallet.

All the loss. Every one of his sweet smiles. Every time that he'd tease me, when we'd exercise, or when we were just working on the rig together.

All of those memories welled to the surface, threatening to drown me.

We had been so close. Closer than brothers. Closer than blood.

Right before he'd passed, the two of us felt like we were on the cusp of something more. Tiptoeing into new territory. If we'd only had a little more time. Just another conversation. We'd been hanging on the verge of putting something into words. Something within reach, that even now I felt like I could just stretch out my hand and be able to grasp it.

Tycho was a man, so full of life and passion, he was vibrant with it.

He should still be here with me.

Not buried and cold. Nothing but food for the worms.

Taking a deep breath wasn't enough. Not to calm the well of feelings, too big to contain. Not enough to soothe them into something manageable.

"That was Tycho." It was all I could manage to say, and even that I'd only uttered in a small voice.

Pandora brushed her small palm in light strokes against my back. Something about that small measure of warmth and comfort allowed everything out. Giving voice to the emotions I'd always kept bottled up and letting them flow.

"When I lost my pack I didn't feel like I had any options. Everyone was expecting me to stay strong. To pick up the pieces of my life and start over. Form a new pack, just continue being the crew chief. I put on a strong face, it was what everyone expected of me. What I expected of myself. But the only thing that I wanted to do was follow my brothers. It was just so empty in my head. After being so connected, after feeling every single moment of their joy, their sadness. All of it. The last thing that I could feel through the bond was the pain of Tycho dying. Just that last moment of fear, and a flash of pain when he realized what was happening to him. The emptiness... the only thing worse for me than the emptiness was the thought of replacing the bond. Finding new recruits. I loved firefighting, I did. But firefighters are always bonded alphas. I know it sounds stupid, but I felt like if I made a new pack, it would mean that my brothers were truly gone. Like I was erasing all of the evidence that they were ever here."

Pandora slipped her hand into mine, interlacing our fingers with her soft touch. "Nothing that you're feeling is stupid."

I closed my eyes, to shut out that soft look on her lovely face, "I don't think that they'd want me to live like this."

It was the first time I'd admitted it out loud. An antsy feeling that had been growing inside of me for years. Just waiting for this moment to rear its ugly head.

But at the same time, the words felt true.

I can't help but think that if they were out there somehow, in some form, looking down on me, that maybe they'd be disappointed in me. After all the work that we'd done together, rising through the ranks, I'd just given up on being a firefighter. Stopped everything. Abandoned my training, and the people in the city who needed me.

I shook my head. There were just so many hours of training.

The Lee pack had a reputation as the best firefighters in the county. We'd rescued so many civilians... People counted on us. People owed their lives to us.

Then I'd just gone and thrown it all away.

She cocked her head at me, "would you judge them for having a hard time without you?"

My response got stuck in my throat. Those words were too heavy. Carrying more than they could bear. I couldn't swallow them down.

I shook my head. Of fucking course not. How could I ever judge them for this? No one should have to experience this sort of pain.

They had no idea. Not one single idea how hard it was. They didn't know how it felt to have your soul so intimately inter-twined. Then having that connection brutally snapped. Fuck anyone who would stoop so low as to judge.

Oh.

That was exactly the point that Pandora was making.

I hadn't even noticed that along with the weight of loss, I'd been carrying the load of my own self disgust. I hadn't noticed—only reacting to being crushed under it.

Fuck that asshole who was judging the poor guy who had lost his entire pack—Fuck *me*.

Pandora brushed her slender hand along my cheek. "How did you do it? How did you keep holding on?"

"The cat was hungry. No one else was there to feed the little guy."

Pandora looked at me as if she really saw me. Biting her lip as she nodded.

It didn't really make sense, but it was the truth.

I stared off into the ceiling, as if I was looking into the great beyond. As if I'd see them up there somewhere, and they could wave down at me. "We rescued Fireball right before the call where I lost my pack. They'd wanted to keep him... I didn't even like cats. But they were gone, they weren't there to care about him. So, I did it for them."

She leaned in close, whispering the words into my ear as if she was telling me the sweetest secret, "I'm so happy that you're here." She sniffled, and I looked over to her to see the red rimming her lovely eyes. The light trickle of a tear easing its way down her chin.

I heard the words that she'd left unspoken. I'm happy that you are *still* here. That you kept on going, fighting through the darkness. Fighting until I got through to the other side.

Where I met her at the end of it.

"I love you."

The words just slipped out of my lips, escaping from where they were meant to be locked away until the right amount of time had passed. When my girl would be ready to hear them.

"I..." she said.

I opened my mouth. To do what? I wasn't sure. Not to take them back. I couldn't do that, because the words were true.

Maybe to tell her that I didn't need to hear it back. That I could wait for her.

My girl beat me to it.

"I didn't think that I was going to find anyone that I wanted to be with. I thought I was going to be alone. Until I met you."

She sniffed louder than her elegant norm, swiping at the tear that continued to fall. "We need to buy that cat more treats."

I tipped her chin up, so that my lovely girl was facing me once more. Without thinking about it, my lips crashed into hers, drowning all of my loss and loneliness in the sweet taste of the one who had brought me back to life.

TWENTY-TWO
PANDORA

"You can call me Panda. Mother and Father only ever call me Pandora when they are angry at me."

"Panda."

I loved the way he said my name. There was nothing soft about it on his sinful lips, as he infused each syllable with a dark promise. The way he made the sound deep and rumbly as if it was a delicacy and he was ready to savor me bite by bite.

He was watching me with heat in his eyes, hot enough to scorch through my outfit, burning it straight off my skin. His gaze traced across my body like he wanted to feast on every inch of me.

Maybe I should have been embarrassed how he turned my panties into a drenched ruin. How he'd so quickly turned me into this wanton creature that craved him. How I wanted him in me.

Now that I had a taste of his body, and how it felt inside of me. Moving within me. Higher and higher until I felt my peak.

I wanted him.

There was something powerful in knowing that I wasn't alone in this desire. That he wanted me just as much as I wanted him. I could see it in the heat in his eyes. The way that he seemed to hold his breath as I stretched. How his hot gaze would linger on my curves. Drinking me in.

I shivered, as the heat of his gaze shuddered down the full length of my spine. Drawing me in closer. As if he had me all tied up in invisible strings and he was pulling me in closer.

Closer.

I leaned in, my gaze drawn to his mouth.

He didn't make me wait.

He didn't make me ask for it.

Instead, he took all of that wanting inside of me and magnified it into something more. Something burning and brilliant between the two of us as his lips crashed down into mine.

His kisses made me desperate. The way that he moved his mouth against mine, sent heat flooding through my lower belly. Awakening something within me.

I had to have him closer. Wrapping my arms around his neck and up into the fine stands of his hair, I kissed him greedily.

Mitexi pulled me into his lap as he sat on his bed. I quickly moved to straddle him.

We both gasped at the friction, as I ground against his hardness.

Mitexi slid rough hands down my back and along my sides, finding the hem of my chemise and then slipping his fingers under it. Rough hands slid over my flat stomach and up. Up to the soft swells of my breasts, which were becoming full and achy as he touched me. Close, but not quite where I needed him.

I whined, needy, and Mitexi relented. Slowly, slowly he slid his hands up, cupping my breasts, and twisting my aching nipples. Those rough hands were perfect against my sensitive peaks. The way that he was tugging was just right. The perfect friction to leave me flooded with slick. Utterly drenched for him.

Mitexi was kissing along my neck, pressing in hard, nipping me.

Was this it?

Was he going to bond me?

Shivers erupted down the length of my spine, leaving me feeling dizzy with pleasure.

"Yes," I moaned.

Helpless.

He could do anything to me. Anything at all. I was his. Completely.

But then his lips drifted against my shoulder blades, pressing a trail of kisses along my sternum.

The omega part of me was losing her mind. It took everything in me to hold back from begging him to bite me. I needed his mark on me. His teeth in me. I needed his claim to break through my skin, marking me so everyone would know exactly who I belonged to.

So no one could ever take me away from him.

"Mitexi," his name on my lips was a plea, "I'm yours."

His response was borderline feral. Growling so deep I could feel the rumble of it in his chest. He shoved me down, bearing his weight over me. Yanking my chemise off and tearing down both my leggings and lace panties, shoving them to the floor. The moment my breasts were bared, he latched on, sucking hard. My back arched off the bed, pressing my chest closer as he devoured me. As he switched breasts, my nipples were left tingling and sensitive in the cool air.

As he laved at my breasts, his other hand grasped my bent knee, brushing down the length of my thigh down to my hips. Tugging me closer against his hardness, keeping me well acquainted with the shape of his arousal.

"I got you, Panda," he murmured between kisses.

There wasn't an inch of me that he hadn't touched. Kissed and licked. Caressed. Every part of me had been loved by him.

Every touch—rough and demanding, to gentle and

worshiping—each one felt as if it was smoothing away the past. All of his praises and desire sunk into me. Replacing everything I'd gone through, until it was as if my body had never been hurt at all.

As if he was easing me out of the chrysalis and helping me fly.

His gray eyes were hot and fixed on mine, and he pulled his shirt up and over his head. Revealing a torso that was sculpted and perfect. Something that deserved to have a likeness made in marble and placed in every museum in the world.

But that wasn't going to happen. All of his chiseled and raw strength—it was all just for me.

Then he tugged his pants all the way down his legs, releasing his cock. He was so big. So hard that once released, his arousal slapped against his abs, pointing straight to the ceiling.

Mitexi stroked my inner thighs, in downward strokes until he reached my core. Where he stroked along my clit in a circular pattern that made me gasp.

Mitexi plunged his finger deep into me. Humming in appreciation when he felt how absolutely drenched I was.

"You're so wet for me," he praised, as he dragged his finger up and down the length of my walls.

The friction of his finger within me was a tease, giving me just enough to make me desperate for what I was missing.

"I need you," my voice was a whine. A desperate plea for the pleasure that was just out of reach. That only he could give me.

Mitexi slipped his finger out of my aching center, and settled over me. Taking my mouth in a rough kiss, his tongue plunging into my mouth, twining with mine. Creating a friction that was driving every thought straight out of my head.

"Baby girl, I'm going to take care of you," he crooned, cradling my face in his large palm.

I nodded, biting my lip.

Yes.

He was going to take care of me. He was going to make me feel *so good*.

Mitexi reached down, grasping his big cock and moving it into position. I could feel the prodding at my entrance, as he notched within me. Then the pressure and bliss as he pushed, filling me completely. Stretching and accommodating me into someone who existed for his pleasure. Into someone who was desired. Loved.

Mitexi groaned, the sound was deep and sent shivers fluttering in my lower belly.

"Fuck, baby," he moaned, "you feel so fucking good."

He moved within me carefully, as if I was made out of porcelain. As if I was a delicacy and he moved slowly to savor me. "Tell me how you want it."

I loved the careful way that he worshiped me, but that wasn't what I needed.

I needed more.

"I want all of you. Take me hard."

His eyes dilated as my words hit him, darkening as his pupils bloomed.

He kissed me gently on the temple, once. Then he started to *move*.

He fucked me like a beast. Like a force of nature rather than a man. Each stroke was fast and brutal as he took me with everything he had. Unleashing an onslaught of passion, fucking me like he was desperate. Like he needed me. Like he would die if he couldn't shove himself deeper into me. Hard and fast.

Just how I needed it.

I arched my back, whimpering. Canting my hips to take him deeper, grasping his broad back in my hands hard enough to leave scratches.

He felt impossibly good. Moving within me. On top of me. His muscular arms braced on either side of me. Gazing at me with adoration. Pressing against something sensitive within me, while his torso pressed right against my clit, grinding against me with each thrust.

I was so close. My body was vibrating right at the edge of a precipice. All I wanted was to fall. To lose myself to the sensation. I just needed a little more. More pressure, more friction. My hand drifted down, seeking out my pleasure.

Mitexi intercepted my drifting hand, twinning my fingers with his. He brought my knuckles up to his lips, kissing them gently, before pressing my hand to the bed. Holding it firmly in place.

"Not yet," he murmured. "Stay with me."

I wanted to squirm, and seek out that friction—rock against his body until I came apart at the seams. But I didn't. Holding myself back. Trusting him.

Being put into this position, being restrained in the same way that... they did. But now being held down by someone who loved me...

I felt safe. I never thought that I'd be okay with being held down.

Never expected to want this. To have this feel so good.

Then Mitexi began rotating his hips in a circular motion that felt so damn good. My head fell back against the pillow, as his thrusts chased away every thought in my mind. Replacing every thought with *yes*. And *please*. And for God's sake, *more*.

The way that he was thrusting into me. How his knot was starting to thicken. The fat girth was making every stroke, every motion more intense.

I needed him to keep doing that.

My mouth fell half open. To beg him not to stop. To keep going. Just like that. Exactly like that. Only it felt too good, and the only thing that came out of my mouth was a helpless throaty moan.

Even without me saying a word, he didn't stop. He kept pressing into me. Grinding against me. Circling his hips just right.

He groaned deep and desperate, as he began to quicken his pace. All of his movements started to feel more intense. Faster, and so deep, and so good.

Too much pleasure for me to hold.

Until I couldn't take it anymore—I shattered as I came.

Stars burst behind my eyelids, as every inch of my body broke apart into white hot bliss. I came so hard that my eyes rolled back, and my legs shuddered.

Mitexi slammed into me hard, as I lay panting and boneless. Once. Twice. Then his whole body tensed as he roared his release. I could feel his cock throbbing deep within me, jetting out spurt after spurt of his cum. Then his knot bloomed right behind my hip bone. Locking him into me.

It was all so much.

The waves of contentment bursting from my core, and rolling to each and every one of my limbs. The huge cock that was still pulsing inside of me. The heavy load of his semen, settling in my lower belly.

The handsome man panting on top of me, who watched me with searing adoration in his eyes.

Suddenly, it all became too much.

Too much bliss.

Too much love.

Too much.

Tears. Fat, stupid tears, welled up into the corners of my eyes. Sliding down my cheeks before I could turn to the side or brush them away.

I barely had time to hide them before Mitexi noticed.

"No, baby!" His eyes were wide and panicked, as he cursed under his breath.

Mitexi grasped me around the back, and flipped us around so that I was on top. He soothed his hands up and down my back, trying to comfort me. "I'm sorry. Did I hurt you? Was that too hard?"

I shook my head, both to tell him no, that wasn't it, as much as it was to sort out what exactly I was feeling.

I sniffled, wishing I could drag back all those tears back into my eye sockets, and stop making my man worry.

No. He hadn't hurt me. He was perfect.

So, what was this?

What the hell? Why was I crying?

I placed my hand against his jaw, stroking the tips of my fingers against his cheeks. It all started to click into place.

This emotion overwhelmed me—it wasn't a feeling of hurt. It was a revelation.

I stared into his concerned gray eyes, at his handsome face that was slightly blurred by these stupid tears that just would not stop.

I took a deep breath to steady myself. I had to tell him. He deserved to hear it too.

"I love you," I whispered against his lips.

TWENTY-THREE
PANDORA

"Keep your eyes closed," Mitexi murmured into my ears.

I walked into the room slowly, taking time with each step. Mitexi stood at my back, gently guiding me, with the occasional "almost there."

I could feel the excitement in the air, radiating from the man standing behind me.

I tried to figure out the surprise. Focusing on the excitement, reminding myself that I was safe. This wasn't anything like the last time I was blindfolded. Also I didn't have anything over my eyes other than my own hands. I was doing this because it was my own choice.

Because I trusted him.

At first the only thing I could smell was the rich and spicy scent of cardamom. The delicious aroma of my scent match, with notes of lemon, and the subtle undertone of wood and camphor. My scent match.

It took a minute to parse through the smells, to notice the citrus and smoked paprika and roasted garlic hanging in the air. My lip perked up. Had he made me dinner?

Mitexi had been tinkering around the house, telling me that

he'd been working on a surprise for me. He'd simply smirked at me and repeated that it was a surprise when I'd asked him for more details. I had no idea what he'd been planning. I'd heard the occasional clang of something dropped followed by a muttered curse word coming from the other room, as I'd worked on my emails before he'd come and fetched me.

"Alright, open them," Mitexi whispered into my ear.

Slowly, I lowered my hands to see a romantic dinner set up. The table was set with a crisp white tablecloth, soft candlelight, and a single rose in a vase. Dinner was expertly plated, like I'd expect from a three star restaurant, and it smelled amazing. It was all some of my favorite foods as well. Chicken piccata with a side of garlic herb rice and roasted zucchini. Not that I'd ever discussed with Mitexi what my favorites were, he must have been paying attention as I'd eaten with him when he was on guard duty.

"This is lovely," I bit my lip, trying to rein in the tears welling in the corner of my eyes. I didn't want to seem like the kind of person who just cried over everything. It was just that... no one had gone out of their way to prepare something like this for me before. Sure, my parents had ordered me fine meals. But they'd never prepared me something so intricate on their own.

I rubbed at my eyes in a way that I hoped looked casual. Luckily I'd stopped crying before I'd really started, and I think Mitexi was distracted, making sure that everything was going perfectly. I don't think that he even noticed. Hopefully.

As I stepped to the table, Mitexi pulled the chair out for me, helping me to my seat. I ducked my head down to hide the blush on my face. It was almost silly that a fancy dinner was capable of turning me into a blushing mess. This man had been inside of me, had his face pressed into my pussy, eating me out until he'd had me shrieking. So... why was something simple like getting a chair pulled out for me enough to make me turn red? Still?

He seated himself across from me. "Please, help yourself."

I cut myself a portion of the chicken. Vowing to be appreciative, even if it was dry and over seasoned. I needn't have worried. The chicken was juicy and buttery soft. Practically melting in my mouth, and well seasoned.

I couldn't help it, the food was so good, it had me biting back a moan. "You never told me you could cook?"

He just shrugged, casually. A smirk on his handsome face.

Everything was delicious. The zucchini was soft, with a slight crunch on the outside, and a subtle floral flavor. The garlic rice had just the right amount of butter. Made with basmati rice, the dish was soft and fluffy. He'd even paired the meal with my favorite rosé wine. White Zinfandel. Choosing the one I preferred, even though the piccata sauce called for a drier drink.

The two of us ate in mostly comfortable silence. Mitexi left me to carry the conversation, which was fine. He looked like he was mentally wrestling with something. Swallowing nervously. Watching me when he thought that I wasn't looking, then quickly averting his gaze when I looked up.

Okay. He'd never done that before.

Maybe Mitexi was feeling uncomfortable? Having second thoughts about inviting me into his home now that I was actually here.

That was understandable. He'd been living alone for years, and all of a sudden he'd had his bachelor pad invaded... It was a lot to process. Especially since most of the rooms were already being used for him to hold on to memories of his pack. Now that I was here, was my presence demanding him to sacrifice part of his safe space?

I couldn't do that to him—we'd only really been together for like a week. I was overstepping some major boundaries.

Was I pushing this relationship further than what he was ready for?

Sure he told me that I could stay, and he cooked me an amazing meal, but did that mean that he wanted me around all the time? He hadn't even agreed to bond with me... refused to even be paid to do it.

Maybe he simply wasn't ready for something that serious.

Bonding was an even bigger deal than marriage.

Besides, Mitexi had gone silver status. He'd chemically castrated himself from other alphas in order to avoid the bond. Why should I assume that he'd want to connect in that way with me?

If he didn't want to bond with me, what did that mean? What were we doing? Was he just sleeping with me, until he got bored with me? It's not like I had any relationship experience. What if I was being too needy and he didn't know how to tell me?

Should I go back home?

Right.

Go back to the same house where I'd been attacked days ago.

Go back to staring at the walls at night.

Go back to lying in bed with my brain wide awake. Whenever I managed to get more than five or so minutes of sleep—jolting awake. Panicked. Sure that someone was going to break in and take me away.

Or I could try to find another place to stay. Without the only bodyguard I'd ever been able to trust. Because I'd fucked my body-guard and any chance of having a semblance of a normal life along with it.

How about I just put another advertisement out for a new bodyguard and cross my fingers that I don't get an anxiety attack and end up hospitalized again?

I was catastrophizing. Over basically nothing. All Mitexi had done was briefly avoid eye contact for a few minutes and my thoughts had started to spiral out of control.

Why was I like this?

Besides the sleep deprivation... and my post-traumatic stress disorder. Obviously.

If my therapist was here, I'm sure that she would have things to say.

"You okay?" Mitexi's deep voice broke through my thoughts. He was staring at me. What had I been doing? I'd been dissociating, maybe staring out into nothing. "You got sort of pale."

"Yeah," I shook my head, as if that would dislodge the thoughts before they could take hold once more. "It's nothing," I muttered.

I was eating a really nice dinner, with my scent match who had always been patient and kind to me. There wasn't any reason to panic.

"There's something I'd like to ask you," Mitexi grasped my hand in his, intertwining our fingers. Mine were dwarfed in his much larger hands. He took a deep breath, his eyes fixed on where his hands held mine. "We've only been together for a short while..."

I swallowed reflexively, as something in my stomach plummeted. I'd thought that my fears were just in my head. Was it true? Was I rushing things with him? Mitexi meant everything for me. Being with him had literally changed my life... Did I need him more than he needed me? Had that blinded me to the fact that he didn't need me the same way that I needed him?

Mitexi brushed my knuckles with his thumbs as he continued, "but already I couldn't imagine my life without you. You're it for me."

Where before I felt weighed down, bracing myself for the rejection that I was sure was going to hit me... now it was as if the floor had been ripped out from under me and I was spinning into free fall.

"Mitexi." I whispered his name.

"If you feel the same way, I don't want to spend any more time without making you mine. Officially, I mean." He stared into my eyes, letting me feel the heat of his gaze. As if each word that he spoke was burned into me. "However you want, I can make that happen. If you want the princess bond, I'll give you a princess bond. If you want a regular bond, I can do that. Whatever you want."

I looked away from him as my face heated up and moisture welled up in the corner of my eyes, threatening to spill over. He lifted up my chin, until I was looking at his handsome face, blurred through unshed tears.

"I love you," he murmured as he brushed away the tears that escaped, leaking down my cheek. "If you aren't ready, I can wait for you. As long as you need, I'll be here for you. I just wanted you to know that as soon as you're ready. I want you."

I sniffled. Loudly. My makeup was probably a lost cause, I'm sure that there were streaks of mascara making dark trails along my jaw. If I didn't stop crying, soon enough my face would have enough bars running across it to look like a jail cell. This wasn't how I'd imagined bonding with my scent match would go.

I brushed my eyes, angrily. I was done with crying over getting exactly what I wanted. The man that my heart had been yearning for, honestly since the first moment that I'd met him.

What was stopping me from having him? From being loved, just like anyone else who wanted to be loved. It sure as hell wouldn't be me stopping myself.

I was ready to have him. To accept good things in my life. I deserved that just as much as everyone else.

Mitexi didn't look at me like I was broken. Like I was nothing more than the trash that life spat out. That people didn't quite know what to do with.

I could have this. I could have him.

Slowly, I forced myself to meet his gaze, and face the silent want, all that fiery heat in his stormy gray eyes. He wanted me.

Mitexi never once made me think that I was lesser than for the things that I'd been through. He wanted me just the way that I was.

There was nothing and no one to hold us back.

Slowly I nodded.

"Yes." My voice was a whisper. Barely audible.

As if I was fighting against all of those silent judging faces, that had looked at me and seen less than. As if I was fighting against every single person who turned to whisper, when they thought that my back was turned or that I was out of earshot. Using my story as a cautionary tale. Looking at me and always seeing what I could have been rather than who I was. As if I was nothing but a living shadow of myself.

Mitexi never treated me that way. He was looking at me... as if I was *everything*. As if I was life. As if he was starving and I was the promise of a feast in the famine.

He was looking at me like I was enough. Like it would be enough to have just me.

I cleared out my throat, saying it once more. "Yes," I met his gaze, "I'm already yours."

I brushed my hair away from my neck, exposing my skin. "And I want everyone who sees me to know it."

I was watching his eyes as I spoke, how they darkened. How they were almost lidded and hazy with something like lust. Something like desperation. Something that ran so hot that I could feel it in my blood. That it made my heart beat faster, pounding like a drum, like the hoofbeats of a mare in heat when he was the stallion. He came closer, until I could feel the press of his lips against my skin, as he kissed me tenderly. Gently. The touch of his lips was the most gentle caress.

Like I was precious to him.

Beneath the kiss, I felt the edge of teeth pressing in deep. Breaking through the skin of my neck.

I'd almost been dark bonded once before. It felt like someone had tried to shove shadows inside of me. Pressing me down and smothered by his desire, until I was almost crushed by it.

This was so much different.

He was offering the princess bond. The best of the three bonds an omega could be offered. One reserved for scent matches.

This bond felt crisp and cool, like the first snowflakes in winter, sparkling and shimmering and transforming everything it touched. Coating everything in soothing sweetness. I felt the lightness of it wrap around me. It was like the feeling of comfort, wrapping all the way around me, like a cozy blanket, wrapping me up, enveloping me in its protection.

The bite at my neck pulsed with a steady beat, and with each of its throbs I could feel it raising me up. It was as if I was floating, soft as a cloud, and the only thing tethering me to the earth was his claim on my neck.

It should have been painful, but instead my body was registering it as the most wonderful thing ever, as my clit throbbed, and wetness spread along my thin lace panties.

I clenched my eyes tight as I whimpered.

The bite had me right on the verge of coming.

All at once, where there had been emptiness, the part of me that had always been lonely.

I felt him.

His emotions swirled beneath the surface of my mind.

I could feel the bond within me. More than simply breaking through the skin of my body, I could feel his presence within my mind. It was like the strumming of an instrument, vibrating in the corners of my consciousness. With each beat of it, I could feel him. It was like a room within my mind was opened, and within it there was nothing but adoration, ever present. And an undercurrent of something darker.

Drowning in the sensation, I gasped.

I could feel his desire. His need for me... pulsing hot. Like a physical presence. I was flooded with him. All of the lonely recesses in my mind... that darkness was now filled with him. Filling me more surely than when he was thrusting inside of me, coating the walls of my pussy with his cum.

I could feel his want. Like a hunger, that he'd barely been able to satiate.

His teeth were at my neck, that were just barely holding back. I could feel how much he wanted more. How much he was desperate to take.

He wanted me.

He wanted me right damn now.

As his teeth slipped out of my neck, I could still feel his presence inside of me. Inside of my mind, in an ever present beat, as consistent as a heartbeat, pulsing with his want.

I could feel just how much he'd been holding back.

Already the skin around my neck felt like it was beginning to cool. Mitexi pressed an open-mouthed kiss where he'd bonded me. Laving my neck. With each sweep of his tongue, I could feel something like devotion.

I was bonded.

I was wanted.

No one would ever be able to hurt me again. Because of him. Mitexi was more than just my scent match... he was my alpha. Strong, and wonderful.

The omega within me whispered, *he'd protect me.*

My hands were shaking with it. Half poised at the button at my chemise, ready to pluck it loose. Ready to bare my body to him just in the same way that I had laid my soul bare. Ready to let him take all of me. Fill me with his claim, just as he had filled me with his bond.

"Are you okay?" Mitexi murmured. His hands traced along my back. "I didn't hurt you?"

He wasn't capable of hurting me. He'd only scratched the surface of things that I wanted him to do to me. The bond revealed a dark promise, and I wanted to hold him to it. I wanted him to deliver.

In answer, I held my hand out to him tentatively. Reaching out until I could feel the firm bunch of his muscles beneath my fingertips. He closed his eyes contentedly under the stroke of my palm, like he was nothing but a large kitten himself. Luxuriating in my touch.

"I feel you," he was in my mind as much as he was in my heart.

I was new to this whole bond thing, but I could sort out the emotions that he was feeling right now. His emotions were smoky, almost heady. Thick with his desire.

"You want me?" I hated that my voice still made it sound like a question. Even now, when he was inside of my mind. When I could feel his desire as strong as I could feel my own.

"I always want you." Mitexi murmured. "Ever since the first moment that I saw you, I've wanted you. All the time," he stroked a strand of my hair back. "You can just ignore it if it's bothering you. I'm a grown man. I can wait."

I bit my lips, as warmth flooded into my lower belly. Desire rose to the surface in me, so strong that I was shocked that he couldn't feel it coursing through the bond. "What if I don't want to wait?"

Mitexi's eyes darkened as got to his feet. Abandoning his plate as a different hunger took over.

"Fucking God, I love you so much," Mitexi growled, as he pressed his lips to mine in a hot kiss.

TWENTY-FOUR
PANDORA

Mitexi kissed me, and kissed me. Hot kisses, tasting of want and friction, and desire on his tongue.

Along with the press of his lips, the warmth of his breaths puffing hot on my cheek, I could feel the bond—all of his desire echoed in my mind. Searing hot.

He scooped me into his arms, holding me with a smile. "Come. There's something I got for you."

As he walked, Mitexi brushed his thumb against my back as he held me.

The friction of his rough calluses holding me, the steady thudding of his heart in his chest, beating at my back. I'd never felt so supported.

He shifted me in his hold as he opened one of the doors that until now I'd assumed was a closet.

He opened it wide, revealing a space that was soft and cozy. A luxurious mattress on the floor. A comforter that looked plush as a cloud, in my favorite shade of lavender. It even had strings of soft fairy lights, twinkling like stars.

I recognized what it was meant to be immediately.

Mitexi had built me a nest.

I opened my mouth to tell him, wait. To tell him that I couldn't... Thank you for the nest, it was really lovely... but... I might. I could...

I froze. Paralyzed as he gently walked me into the room, shutting the door behind him with his foot.

The four walls of the nest pressed in. Closing around me.

I went very still. I think that Mitexi was talking to me, but I couldn't hear him. Could only see his lips moving. It was like I was trapped within a fog. As the air blurred around me, and a haze descended on my mind. Like I wasn't a part of the world. An observer plopped down into it, but not really a part of it.

Unable to say a single word as he lowered me down to the mattress.

I couldn't feel the pillows at my back. Nothing but that scratchy old carpet.

It was as if I was dropped straight into my past. Into that dank closet that they'd kept me locked in. Night after night. Alone with the scratching of cockroaches skittering about. Always listening, and dreading the footsteps of someone. Never sure what they were going to do to me. When they were going to hurt me again.

The roaring in my ears pounded hard, drowning out everything.

Until I was left hurt and lonely. Trying and failing with each passing moment to hold on to hope that somebody was going to find me. That they had to be searching for me.

That was all before I'd perfumed, and that door opened once more to too many hands... holding me down.

All I could hear was my name. Echoing. Like I was hearing it through layers of water. Louder. More urgently. Gradually hearing the words more clearly like I was rising to the surface.

"Pandora!" Mitexi had grasped both of my shoulders.

His cool gray eyes were wide, and scrutinizing mine.

"Panda, are you okay?"

"I'm fine," I lied.

I turned away so he wouldn't notice the heat in my cheeks. Those eyes that didn't miss anything.

"You're shaking." One of Mitexi's large rough hands trailed down my arms.

"I-I."

"We don't have to do anything that you don't want to do."

I shook my head.

No. That wasn't it at all.

"No, that's not it." I didn't want him to walk away thinking that I hated his gift for me. "It's just too tight. The last time I was in a space like that was back when. It was…"

I could not bring myself to say the words.

To mention the closet where my kidnappers had raped me. Tearing away any semblance of safety that I'd still managed to hold on to after they'd stolen me.

"Shit," Mitexi said under his breath, scooping me in his arms once more. He carried me up and out of the room, not stopping, until he had laid me on his own bed, and scooted under the covers next to me. Stroking my back trying to comfort me.

He didn't move. Waiting patiently, as my breaths calmed back down to normal, and the panic faded to quiet shame.

My Alpha had set up a nest for me. A thoughtful and lovely nest. And how had I reacted? A full blown panic attack.

"I'm sorry."

"This isn't your fault. You don't have anything to apologize for."

"It's not that it wasn't a nice nest. It was my favorite color and everything…"

The problem was not the nest. Back before that day… I would have loved the nest Mitexi had made. It was exactly the sort of nest that girls dreamed about. If I had seen the nest he had made in a magazine, I would have probably circled it, or cut out the page when I was younger to save it.

Mitexi nodded like he understood.

"What was your nest like back at your place?" He was staring up at the ceiling, frowning.

I pinched my lips into a thin line, turning away from him. This wasn't a conversation I'd wanted to have with him. I had hoped it would have taken him longer to work it out.

"I didn't. I couldn't. I wanted to have a nest, I did. But every single one. Every time I tried, this happened."

"But omegas need nests."

I nodded. It was a biological truth. But I had realized my own truth a long time ago, that my nest, was never a room at all. I would likely never feel safe in a small room again.

"My nest wasn't a place. I kept it in a security panel in the room I used for my heats."

"It was an item? Something that you left behind in your room? We can always go back for it."

I shook my head, my cheeks coloring, as I admitted the truth to him. "My nest was my gun."

Mitexi inhaled sharply, before he turned toward me on the bed, holding my face gently in his hands. "Hey, hey. Look at me. You don't need a gun. You don't need to be the strong one anymore. You have me. I promise you, with everything that I am. I promise you that I'm going to find who hurt you. I'm not going to stop until I make them pay for it."

As soon as Mitexi spoke the words out loud... it clicked. The reason why I hadn't been able to sleep, why I'd stopped feeling safe.

I thought it was all because someone had broken into my house. But it was more than that. When I wasn't able to fire my gun to protect myself...

My gun was more than a weapon. It had been my assurance that I would never let anyone hurt me. Never again.

But when my gun didn't fire it stopped being my nest. I had been left alone. Defenseless.

It was just another sad reminder of how broken I had let myself become.

I didn't even trust myself, and my own promise that I could protect myself by any means necessary.

Mitexi pulled me closer, holding me so tight I could feel the bulge of each one of his tense muscles as he held me desperately.

"You've been such a good girl. So fucking strong. You've gone through more than anyone should have ever gone through. I know that it doesn't feel like it's over, but I can promise you this. They will never hurt you again. They are never going to touch you. I will make sure that they will never hurt you, or anyone else ever again. I promise you that I am going to find out exactly who did this to you. I am going to fucking end them."

When I looked into the blazing heat in his eyes, for the first time I could feel the truth in his words. As the promise he'd made sunk in deep. No one was ever going to hurt me again. Mitexi would never let that happen. He'd already smashed through locked doors, ripping apart someone who'd tried... my alpha.

Maybe I hadn't been able to save myself. But my alpha? He was strong enough for the both of us. He'd never let anyone hurt me.

TWENTY-FIVE
MITEXI

She was ethereal.

Irresistible.

And all mine.

The princess bond I had given her was already starting to heal. The redness around the edges was already fading into something light and almost shimmery. The edges rather than looking like scars were almost crystalline, like the edge of a snowflake. Far prettier than any bite should have the right to look like.

As gold pack omegas were frowned upon in society, people didn't always say the quiet part about them out loud. That there was something more to them. As though they were magnetized and larger than life.

That it was harder for alphas to ignore the pull of a gold-pack omega.

All omegas were a biological cocktail that lured alphas in. Alphas would protect an omega without consciously deciding to do so. It was written into our DNA, into our very blood. It all had to do with genetics, and being physically attracted to a partner most likely to be able to create more alpha offspring. The pheromones of an omega had alphas chemically wrapped around their fingers.

Omegas were biologically designed to draw alphas in, and alphas were hardwired to want to protect them.

It was actually a full unit in the first responder class, on the alpha drive to protect omegas. As most of the civilian population was beta, in the case of a fire if the majority of alphas went in blindsided by their instinct to protect an omega in need, it would put civilians at risk.

You couldn't have a team of four alphas all rushing in to save the same omega in the building while neglecting every single other civilian. It had happened enough to be documented. Crew chiefs especially had to directly instruct their squad where to go. Because if alphas trusted their instincts, they would head straight to the omegas every time.

Before Pandora, I'd never really spent a great deal of time around a gold-pack omega. But I had heard rumors about their influence.

Although Alphas never publicly admitted it, it was generally understood that gold-pack omegas were more. More sensual. More compelling. Gold pack omegas had that same chemically seductive quality, but on steroids.

People tended to twist it around, make it seem like there was something toxic and perverted about a gold-pack omega's sensuality.

Maybe I'd been out of the loop and isolated from polite society for too long, but I just didn't give a flying fuck.

I was more than happy to live in that corner of my mind that others deemed as irresponsible or perverted. I wanted to drown in my attraction to her.

It wasn't as if I had any responsibility to monitor myself anymore. There was no emergency fire where I had to keep my need for her in check in order to save everyone. I was completely at liberty to drown in her essence. In the heady chemical cocktail that was forever beckoning to me. Drawing me in and leaving me reeling.

But one factor that I hadn't taken into consideration, when I'd bonded Pandora was how the princess bond, more than a regular bond, intensified that instinct to protect her.

It made sense. The princess bond elevated the omega. Pandora deserved nothing less. It wasn't even that she had been through enough and deserved a happily ever after.

Pandora was fucking divine. She was literally the most beautiful woman I'd ever seen in my life. With a face that was almost too angelic to be real, and a body that was all lush curves that were specially designed to make me lose my mind. From the first moment I'd seen her I had barely tried to avoid her. Even when it came at the risk of my job. Tearing apart the professionalism instilled into me from as far back as I could remember.

I had no idea how I'd managed to end up with a girl like Pandora. She seemed to be too perfect to be real. I don't know what I'd done to deserve her. Honestly, I doubted that I even did. But by some crazy fucking miracle she wanted me. I wasn't going to question it.

There was never a doubt in my mind but to give her exactly what she deserved.

I just hadn't anticipated how the princess bond was going to utterly wreck me.

After the bond snapped into place, I felt her so strongly. I reacted to Pandora's presence like she was a livewire. She was electrifying. An addiction.

Now I could feel the devastating panic in her mind. I could feel her having a breakdown. One that I'd put her into just a few minutes after I'd ever given her the bond. The pure unadulterated fear. Blinding and white-hot and paralyzing when I'd placed her into that stupid nest I'd made for her.

The bitter self-hatred that followed.

She didn't deserve any of it.

Pandora was still so afraid. I'd never heard the full extent of what happened to her, but something in my gut told me that it had to be worse than she let on.

Her pain was so visceral. So raw.

The fact that no one had ever found the men who had done this to her.

It consumed me.

I would make Pandora feel safe again if it was the last thing I did. If it took selling off everything I owned and giving every last scrap of money I'd managed to save.

I would make her feel safe once more.

She was mine.

I was currently curled around her, with a strand of her hair woven around my fingers. Telling my overwrought boner that it was not going to get any for the moment, Pandora had just had a panic attack dammit.

All I wanted to do was press my face deep into her neck and inhale deeply.

Pandora was a drug. I don't know if it was the princess bond, or the fact that she was gold pack. Hell, I might have always responded to her this way. Whatever it was, it didn't really matter.

Pandora had finally fallen asleep after her panic attack.

I wanted to get started reaching out to my contacts, and see if any of my connections could help me find any leads.

But Pandora needed me now. She'd finally gotten to sleep. I'd tried once to slip away from her, to make calls in the other room. As soon as I moved away from her, Pandora started to shift and stir. I stayed by her side—if my baby girl needed me, I wasn't going to deny her. Besides, I could still start some preliminary searches on my phone.

I'd never been more enraged by a simple internet search.

It was odd how I never had searched social media or the internet for Pandora. Not one single time before I had signed up to be her bodyguard. I had no idea that her name was splashed all across the internet in lurid colors. Pandora had never spoken about what had happened to her, but she hadn't needed to tell me a word. It was there with anyone with a wifi connection to see it.

Just the search results when all I'd done was type in her name was enough to make my blood boil.

Most of the news articles I was scouring through all seemed to reference a single source, someone named Sylvia Cambell. A further search named her claim to fame as being the friend who had been kidnapped along with Pandora. Why did she feel free to spill all of Pandora's ordeal?

Because of her, Pandora was in dozens of newspapers. Sensationalized articles, a tell-all from the estranged friend, Sylvia, talked about how her driver had taken the girls from a trip to the mall. How they'd gotten driven out to a run-down warehouse, where a pack of alphas was waiting for them.

It was a gruesome violation of her privacy.

I had to go search out the original interview with Sylvia, because I couldn't believe it. How could she be so callous?

But somehow reading through the original interview was worse.

"Yeah, I don't think that they were supposed to beat her, but they definitely did. I could hear it before they dropped a bag over my head and separated us."

I was sure that I'd read it wrong. I had to read it a third time, before the truth sunk in, aching and awful where it settled somewhere deep in my bones.

The more I read, the more awful the interview became.

"That's not even the worst thing that happened to her. Pandora reached out to me after she was released. She told me everything. How she perfumed, and the man who brought her food couldn't

resist her. He even gathered others to hold her down, and they all took turns. At least until their lead-alpha forced them to stop."

"Do you think that's what led her to refuse going to the Institute?"

"Well Pandora was always hungry for attention. Going gold-pack is probably her way of staying relevant. She might have been worried that no one would want her after all those nasty men had used her."

**Interviewers here at Steamy Aura's Weekly reached out, but the Delano family declined to make any official statement.*

I would have shattered my phone against the wall if I wasn't worried that it would wake Pandora up. I had to force myself to loosen my grip on her, as I'd unconsciously gripped her harder. It was surprising that I hadn't managed to wake her.

What the hell was up with this so-called friend? What kind of person just went out and blabbed about someone's abuse? Just went and made it all high profile and public knowledge for anyone who wanted a bit of cheap entertainment?

Not a friend any longer, considering how Pandora had never mentioned her.

Pandora was so elegant, and every one of her family members treated me with nothing but dignity and respect. Seeing her history splashed all over these cheap magazines, and shady websites was fucking maddening. It was disgusting.

It felt as though I had opened up the can of worms, reaching in and touching the writhing and slimy bodies. Now I couldn't stop. Not until I got to the bottom of it all.

TWENTY-SIX

MITEXI

The sooner I could get my hands on the people who had harmed her, the better. Any moment when her kidnappers were left free was too long. They'd already caused enough pain. I wasn't about to let them poison the world by being allowed to run free in it.

I would make sure that Pandora got justice.

"Would you like me to call in a favor? I could have a law enforcement team monitor our security cameras while I'm out."

"Can you drop me off at my parent's house?" She asked in her lovely voice. She always managed to sound elegant and level-headed, though I could feel through the bond the anxiety she could barely keep at bay.

I swallowed my frustration. I'd been in such a rush to get started, and hunting down leads, I hadn't even considered what kind of impact it would have on Pandora to leave her here alone. "If you aren't feeling safe, I could hold off the meeting. I'll make sure to put up more security features. I'll buy more advanced locks and find a place to install a panic room."

"No that isn't it at all." Pandora shook her head, frowning. "I just need to talk to my parents about something."

"Oh." She seemed awfully nervous through the bond. Was it

from the thought of going back to her house alone? "Do you need me to go with you?"

Pandora sighed, pinching the bridge of her nose between her thumb and index finger. "No. This is something I need to do on my own."

As I dropped her off in front of her parent's house, I had to shut down my own irrational instincts to go running after her.

The last time I'd been in a car watching Pandora walk away from me, was right before her heat. Right before she'd been attacked.

No one was going to ever be able to hurt her again. Not ever.

I needed to go. To make sure that what happened to her would never be repeated.

But the only lead that I had was the damn friend.

It wasn't hard to search up her workplace. Not when she'd built her fame off of her tell-all interview exclusive. A simple search on her name brought up the article "Kidnapped Friend Opens Exclusive Boutique."

It was a trendy looking store. Located on the west side of downtown New Oxford. It was one of those boutique stores that rich women shopped at when they wanted to look like a cultured and fancy kind of hippie. There were hand-crafted earrings made out of crystals, and bags with way too much embroidery.

I could recognize the woman sitting behind the glass counter from her interview pictures, even though since then she'd dyed her hair a platinum blonde. She was older, with a harshness around the eyes that wasn't present in the photos from years ago, but still undeniably the same person.

"Hello there, can I help you?" Sylvia Cambell asked in one of those professional voices that sounded unnaturally polite and chipper. "Are you looking for something nice for someone? A gift for your girlfriend?" Her smile stretched wider.

Should I try to play it like I was any old customer? Try to ply her for information? No. I'd probably fuck it up. "I'm Pandora Delano's alpha."

The smile melted off her face, curving into a smirk.

"So Pandora managed to find herself somebody? After everything?" She leered at me, mocking me.

I stared at her blankly. Shocked by her undisguised hatred.

There was no way that this girl was talking about the same Pandora. My Panda was the sweetest thing, and hadn't done anything to deserve being the sole target of all this blind hatred.

It took everything in me to hold myself back from curving both palms into fists.

It didn't even register in my brain that this nasty piece of work was a small and weak woman. All of my first responder training was replaced with rage. I couldn't even say that she wasn't a threat to my omega... because who was the one who had made her so uncomfortable to be out in the rest of society, if it wasn't for her?

I couldn't let her rile me up. I needed the information.

"I'm trying to hunt down Pandora's kidnappers. I'm here to see if you remember any distinct features on any of them? Anything you might have forgotten to mention to this police?"

"You think that kind of information comes without a price?" Sylvia smirked at me, like she was a cat and I had no idea that I was the mouse right in her crosshairs. "You're not the sharpest pencil in the box, now are you?"

"Honestly, you owe it to her after all the shit you've said about her on the internet."

"Owe her? You think I owe her?" Sylvia held a hand to her chest and laughed like I'd come up with the funniest joke ever. "That girl ruined my life!"

I was just about done with this bullshit.

"When did she do that? Did she force you to go to sketchy

magazines and let the whole world know how she was assaulted? In detail?"

"No, I suppose that it was Pandora's father who did that." Sylvia shook her head like she was disappointed. "You know that her asshole of a father wasn't going to pay off my ransom at first? I had nothing to do with any of this. I'm not even an omega, and I was this close," Sylvia got right into my face, holding up her thumb and index finger pinched close together, "to being sold. I heard the kidnappers talking about it. If Pandora hadn't been raped then it would have been me. All because her stupid family and her stupid driver got me into all of this. None of it was my fault."

"So you decided that it was okay to slander her name?" I spoke slowly because I couldn't believe the entitlement of this girl.

"That's the nice thing about being wealthy. No matter what information is out there about her, nothing that's happened to Pandora is going to ever touch her." Sylvia's eyes narrowed. "She never had to live in the public eye after everything. Always shielded from the fallout. Nothing ever got to hurt perfect little Pandora."

"Yes," I made a show of looking around the fancy and over-priced items in her store. "I can see how you're suffering."

Sylvia's face turned red, as she pointed a finger right at me. "You don't understand. You have no idea what it was like. Those men were brutal, and they were going to do the same to me. I'd heard them talking about it. Saying how at least they might get a piece of the less pretty friend. They probably would have done it too if Pandora hadn't ended up perfuming."

"But you weren't. Pandora was the one they assaulted. But for some reason, you're still blaming Pandora. You think that you didn't deserve this... but she did?" I spoke softly, lowering my voice as another piece of my heart broke for my girl.

I'd read in the interview that before they were taken, Sylvia was her best friend.

Pandora had really lost her entire life in one awful day.

"It was nothing personal. It was all business. Mr. Delano couldn't be persuaded to offer a reasonable amount of hush money. So we had to go to someone who was prepared to pay us fairly... Don't look at me like that. None of it was right, none of this should have happened to me. It wouldn't have happened to me if I had just stayed away from Pandora. I never should have been friends with that stupid cunt in the first place."

I snarled at her. I couldn't help it—a growl reverberated through my chest.

Loud. Violent.

I think that Sylvia saw something in my face to clue her in to the fact that I was barely holding myself back from punching her right in her entitled jaw, because she leaned back away from me.

Fuck. I probably shouldn't have done that.

I cleared my throat as if I hadn't just been growling at her, like some dumb animal. "So there's nothing you can remember at all?"

Meeting this bitch was an utter waste of time. Pandora had deserved better friends. Someone who could have shown her a modicum of loyalty. Not this asshole who'd run her mouth, simply because she was angry that it happened, and needed a scapegoat. So Sylvia had gone and made everything ten times worse for my girl.

"Oh, God. You're never going to stop. Fine, I'll throw Pandora's dog a bone. There's one detail that I never mentioned in that news article." She was staring at her nails, inspecting the cuticles, acting like nothing in this conversation was getting to her. "I saw a tattoo on some of the kidnappers."

"A tattoo?"

If more than one of the kidnappers had a tattoo... could it be a gang identifier? Maybe something that could be tracked? Mentioned somewhere in the system?

"I noticed they had tattoos of an ouroboros, though none of them had it in the same spot.

They weren't obvious. One of them had it on their inner wrist. Another man hid it beneath the hair on the back of his neck."

"Can you tell me anything about what he looked like?" I didn't mention who I was talking about. My voice lowered, as I fought to keep the rage out of it.

Sylvia knew exactly who I meant. It was like a shadow crossed her face.

"He had a scar on his hand, between his thumb and index finger. The man who got everyone to rape her." That shakiness in her voice... how her voice got low, as if she was scared that someone might overhear her...

It was a reminder. Even if she had taken all of her anger out on Pandora, pinning everything on her. Justifying what seemed like a senseless betrayal and cruelty...

Sylvia was a victim in this herself.

People did all kinds of awful things to survive.

But the moment passed, and the cruel smirk returned, slipping back on Sylvia's face like a well worn mask.

"Now kindly, get the hell out of my store."

TWENTY-SEVEN

PANDORA

I'd only been away for a few days, and already it felt like I was a stranger walking through the house I'd grown up in.

I shivered, walking through the marble hallway heading in the direction of my Father's study. Wishing that Mitexi was here with me, to put his arm around my shoulders. To be a steady presence at my side. Warming me.

I know that he would have followed me in a heartbeat if I'd asked.

But like I'd told him, this was something that I needed to do on my own. I didn't want to risk having Father put on a mask in front of someone he'd deemed an outsider. No. I needed to hear his explanation, in his own unfiltered words.

If there was a reasonable explanation, I wanted it to come straight from the source.

Mitexi had vowed to find me justice. I was just helping matters along from my end.

It hadn't taken long to notice discrepancies in the security records that monitored my heat room.

There was no way that accessing my heat room should have been that easy. It was designed with layers of safeguards.

There should have been guards posted for 24 hours. Guards with explicit instructions not to let anyone in. There was no way that Daniel should have been able to make his way over to me without being stopped.

Unless someone had given them orders to let them through.

The door to my heat room could only be opened from the outside with a physical key and a code. That metallic clink that I'd heard... the simplest explanation was that somehow he'd gotten a spare key. But even with the key, my door required a four digit code. Anyone entering the wrong one would have set off the alarm.

It was almost as if someone had given him the code directly.

Then again, there was always the possibility that Daniel had become a tech wizard in his spare time, or hired a tech wizard...

Then there was the fact that Daniel was a work associate of Father. I'd done some digging. The two of them had some shared real-estate investments, as recently as four months ago. Whoever Daniel was, Father had known him. Had worked closely with him.

No one should have been able to simply break in.

Daniel hadn't broken in. He'd waltzed through my door.

I steeled myself outside the thick oak door of Father's study. I hadn't called him in nearly a month. I hadn't spoken to him in person in even longer.

When did we become this distant? When I was little I'd spent most nights at least having dinner with my parents. We'd spoken every day. Watching movies like any normal family.

I'd been so lost in my own issues, I'd hadn't seen how relationships were shattering all around me.

As I knocked lightly, and let myself in, Father looked up at me briefly, before returning to his paperwork. "Panda darling, what brings you here?"

Silently, I held out the printouts I'd brought with me. The

entire seventeen pages of records from my heat room, with each discrepancy highlighted. I waited, practically holding my breath, until he noticed, frowning.

He took the papers from me, looking over the records with a sigh.

"Father, do you know anything about this?" My voice was only just above a whisper, as if a part of me didn't want to know the answer.

Which was ridiculous. Because what I suspected... it couldn't be true. There was no way. I had gone through trauma and sometimes I didn't see things clearly. There had to be another explanation.

Father locked his clear blue eyes on me. "It seems like you already know what it means."

I gazed, wide eyed. Not comprehending.

"Father?"

No. It couldn't be. He would never.

He'd seen what had happened to me after the kidnapping and the...rape. He was enraged on my behalf. Had wanted to find out who'd done it, even offered a cash reward for any news.

He would never be behind this.

So why was he saying that he was?

"Father? You?"

"What was I supposed to do?" Father snapped at me. "My daughter just gave up on life and I was supposed to just let that happen? That's like giving up on you. I had to do something, even if it was to force you to start living again."

All I could do was stare at him. Frozen and mute, as inside myself I could feel something vulnerable inside of me fracturing all into pieces. I just stared, with my mouth open and gaping like a fish drowning on land, somehow standing upright, as within me, my heart fell apart.

The same man who used to give me piggy back rides and

neigh like a horse? Who would wink at me, while ordering up some ice cream after a rough day?

The man who I grew up thinking was the strongest in the world. The one no one could beat.

I never even imagined that he could hurt me like this.

You were the last person in the world who'd ever be the one to betray me.

Yet it was you the whole time.

"You wanted your business partner to... dark bond me?"

No.

"Panda. Daniel said that he was going to try to seduce you. He never had permission to dark bond you. That was a misunderstanding."

No, there had to be another explanation. I had to have read the data wrong. There was no way. My own father couldn't have...

"But you put me into a situation where it could have happened." I couldn't take my eyes away from his stoic blue gaze. Looking for any sign that the news was upsetting for him. That I had interpreted something wrong. That this was all just some sort of big mistake.

There was none.

My voice broke, as all of a sudden the truth of it hit me. "How could you?"

"What did you expect me to do? You were hiding in your room for years. My daughter. My only daughter. An invalid. With no end in sight. Despite the best therapy that money had to offer. I know that I've failed you as a parent. I never should have listened to your mother and allowed you to stay away from the Institute. We never should have let you become gold status. I should have put my foot down years ago."

"You were so disgusted by my gold status that you gave up on me? Decided to offer me up, during my heat... What did you expect was going to happen?" My vision blurred with all the tears that I couldn't stop. No matter how much I needed them to stop. Now that Father was the last person on earth I'd trust to see me vulnerable. "Did you just want your business partner to rape me, or did you want him to dark bond me, too? Take me off your hands, like I'm nothing. Were you so disgraced by my gold status that you decided that it was okay for me to become a rich man's sex slave?"

"Obviously I didn't want my only child to end up as a sex slave," he was yelling, and red in the face.

I didn't recognize this man anymore.

Whoever he was, he wasn't my father. My father wouldn't do this to me.

I wasn't going to argue with him. I didn't even know what to say to him.

The air in here was suffocating me, I couldn't face him any longer.

Which was a shame, because something in me already knew that I wouldn't see my father again. At least, not for a long time.

I turned away from him, blinking away my tears. Forcing myself to not cry. No. He didn't deserve to see me cry. Walking away, and only pausing when I was already halfway out the door.

Without looking back to check to see if he was listening, I spoke in a small voice.

"I am more than what you think of me."

TWENTY-EIGHT
MITEXI

As soon as I was away from the boutique from hell, I was gunning it back to the Delano house. I didn't drive straight to their front door so that their security team would announce my presence, I was just parking nearby in case Pandora needed me.

Once parked, I texted an old contact from work.

> Me: Do you know anyone who'd have access to a database of tattoos that are possibly gang-related?

> Marjorie: Is this Mitexi? Hey! It's been a while, how are you?

Oh, right. I'd been out of the loop for so long, I forgot all about how to make small talk. I backtracked a little with my next text. Marjorie, the sweet-little old receptionist who managed everything behind the scenes at the police department, was always so supportive of me. She always had cookies to give to the squad whenever we used to stop by. She, like everyone else in my life before the accident, completely fell off my social radar.

> Me: I'm doing really well. I found my scent match recently. We just bonded.

> Marjorie: That's so wonderful! I'm so happy to hear that! Congratulations!

> Me:Thank you! It's why I'm asking actually. My omega was hurt by a pack of criminals. I'm trying to track them down to help her feel safe. I'm looking for any reference to snake-ring tattoos.

For two whole minutes there was nothing on my cellphone screen except for three loading dots.

If Marjorie couldn't find anyone, who was left for me to reach out to? It had been a while. The head of the police department owed me one, but was it a good idea to be asking for favors a few days after I was booked at the station? For attempted murder?

I didn't have to dwell on that for long, before Marjorie responded.

> Marjorie: There's nothing coming up in the system, here. Did you try Alex? In the Records Department?

> Me: Thank you Marjorie, you're the best.

I scrolled through my contacts, and somehow AlexRecords was still listed in my phone. I shot him another text, before sitting back down and hunting through all the old names. I'd worked closely with the police department for years. There had to be somebody with the information I needed.

After a few minutes, Alex replied.

Alex: That's not something I have access to, but
I know a guy. He's a hacker and a seer in one. If
those guys farted somewhere on the internet,
my guy will be able to track them down.

Me: Can you send me his contact info?

A phone number labeled 'Kai' popped up on my phone screen.

Alright then. I shot off a hasty text to the hacker—the more times I sent it out the worse the spelling got each time, but whatever—before I got a call.

I frowned, looking at the caller ID, wondering why this guy needed to talk to me directly.

He didn't. It was Pandora on the other line.

I picked it up after one ring.

"Panda?"

"Hey."

I could hear from the sound of her voice that she'd been crying, not that I'd mention anything. Pandora would get embarrassed if I brought it up.

Shit.

Had she gotten freaked out back at her house? I should have insisted on going back there with her.

"Hey, baby. What do you need?"

"How is your trip going?"

Pandora sounded like she was on the verge of a breakdown, and she was just beating around the bush. It had taken me longer than it should have to realize that my girl hated asking for help. She somehow thought of herself as a burden.

Did she have any idea that I would do anything for her?

"I'm done, actually," I said, keeping it casual. "I'm parked just a block away from your house. I can come get you."

"No, no. That's okay. I'll come out and meet you," Pandora insisted.

I could tell from the car, as she walked over to me, that whatever had happened had rattled her. Her eyes were red-rimmed, and she looked shaken, even though she was acting like nothing was wrong as she slipped into the passenger seat.

One look at the determined hunch of her shoulders, and her faraway expression was enough to tell me that she wasn't ready to talk about it.

Instead, I leaned over and grasped Pandora's knee, giving it a squeeze.

"I'm here for you. Whatever you need, just say the word. I'm all ears."

Pandora just shook her head. "I don't want to talk about it. I-" She dipped her head down sharply, holding her forehead in her palm.

I hated seeing her like this.

I reached down, unbuckling her seat belt, and pulling Pandora right into my lap. Just holding her against my chest. She tensed for a moment, before leaning in to me.

I hugged her tighter against me. "Do you want to get out of here?"

"Sorry," she said in a small voice, acting as if she had done something wrong and didn't want to bother me. "We can go back now, I didn't mean to—"

"That's not what I meant. Do you want to go somewhere fun?"

"What? You mean a date?"

I shook my head. "Let's go on a trip. Get away from this city. Whatever's bothering you, fuck it. Let's leave it all behind for now."

"Just like that?"

I shrugged my shoulders, "sure. Why not?"

"Okay," my omega said in a small voice. She pressed her face into my shirt, and I could feel it getting damp.

It wasn't that Pandora was the kind of girl to cry over every little thing. It was just that she was going through some shit right now. She'd gone through more than anyone should ever have to go through. She deserved to have something nice happen to her for once.

Besides, I had a surprise for her. Getting out of the house now would be the perfect time to set it all up.

I drove us straight to the airport, with no bags. No nothing. Screw it, we could get whatever we needed as soon as we got to our destination. As far away as we could get with just our drivers licenses. Using whatever airlines had spare tickets to the nicest places.

It was the off season. People had work. We didn't have any trouble booking something last minute to someplace tropical.

As soon as we got to our seats—splurged and got us business class, which I'd never do for myself, but my girl deserved it— Pandora started to nod off, curled up against my chest with my arm around her.

I accessed the spotty airplane wifi, and sent out emails. Finalizing plans. Sometimes the emails would appear to be sent, before deleting. I'd even caved and updated to the premium wifi, but hey. There was only so much productivity to be had in a flying metal box 35,000 feet in the air. I got enough responses back from the team that it seemed like they got the gist of the plans.

She only started stirring as the flight attendant politely asked me to put my seat into an upright position. My arm was completely numb after being used for the last four hours as her pillow. I was thousands of feet above the clouds, in a metal box that smelled like recirculated stale air and salty peanuts. Then my lovely girl stretched against me.

Nothing had ever felt better.

As soon as she turned it off airplane mode, Pandora's phone started blowing up. 17 missed calls 43 new text messages. She ignored them all, jamming her phone into her pocket like she hadn't even seen it.

If she was prepared to ignore her problems, then I was happy to do the same.

Well, we'd landed someplace tropical and sunny. The perfect place to pretend that none of our troubles existed. It was time to show Panda a good time.

It took her a little coaxing to get her out of her funk. But it all ended up being worth it. The vacation was everything I'd never thought to ask for.

Panda had bought the world's sexiest itty bitty white bikini. The only thing better than getting to see her in it, was helping her put on sunscreen in the hotel room... which led to other things... and ultimately made us two hours late to our dinner reservation by the beach.

Totally worth it.

The water was warm, and at night the shore was bioluminescent. We went wine-tasting and barreling down natural waterslides. Pandora had flatly put her foot down with snorkeling, she was sure that we were going to get eaten by some overgrown fish or something, but I did talk her into a sunset kayaking tour.

Paddling through water that was crystal clear, with a girl who was so fucking gorgeous she had my cock perpetually at half-mast... in a double kayak, gently rocked by the ocean waves. With the sun setting, illuminating the sky in a riot of orange and brilliant pinks that reflected across the flowing water...

Then Pandora turned around, shrieking and laughing, when I'd paddled a little too hard and splashed water all down her front. With a scandalized smirk on her face, she smacked her paddle backwards to get her payback, splashing water all down my legs.

Smiling back at her, it hit me.

I had stopped living... when the rest of my pack had died, a part of me had burned away, lost and buried in the same collapsed rubble that had taken them.

I don't know why I'd decided to live like I was already dead. Didn't even know if it was a conscious decision on my part.

I had spent these last few years right on the cusp of giving up. Having to constantly listen to the emptiness within the bond. Like a phantom limb, constantly itching. With every move that I made, I could feel their loss grating at me. Drowning me.

Before Pandora, I never could never have imagined this day. The pure bliss of making her smile again. That I'd be here with her. That I'd be able to laugh again.

Somehow she'd sunk into the empty pit within my chest, and made me feel. I hadn't had a clue how to put the jagged edges of my broken heart back together.

But it was still beating—it beat for her.

TWENTY-NINE
PANDORA

Coming back from our trip, I was almost relaxed enough to face the mountain of texts from my parents. Not that I was going to.

I'm sure that Mother had finally clued my father in on the fact that I'd moved out—that was if he hadn't already noticed that I'd stopped managing the assets I'd dutifully monitored for years.

Before the last time we'd spoken, it was a given that I'd take over the family business. Eventually. As soon as I got over this trauma, the plan was always to give me more control over the finances and managing the properties. I'd never given them any reason to suspect that I wouldn't continue on with the Delano legacy.

Now?

I just didn't know.

Was it standing up for myself or self sabotage to cut ties?

There was no need to decide right now, in the heat of the moment. Who would I really be hurting if I gave up on the business that was my birthright?

Maybe I was doing this because it was the only way to hurt him back. I was essentially kicking him right where it hurts—his money. His legacy. Any possibility for early retirement.

Maybe I just needed a break. It's not like I didn't enjoy growing my own wealth, and the luxury that came with it.

But for now, I'd let him sweat a little.

I don't remember the last time I'd had a vacation. Even before the kidnapping, my parents had been too busy. It had been years. When Mitexi had suggested that we go, I'd just gone along with it.

Just hadn't realized until we were alone together, somewhere beautiful and new, how much I'd needed it.

On the drive home, Mitexi was looking antsy again.

The last time I'd seen him do that, I'd started spiraling into negative thoughts. Assumed that it had to be something that I'd done.

I swallowed nervously, wrestling with my thoughts like they were a herd of feral kittens and I was standing awkwardly with some catnip and a bit of string in place of a lasso. The last time he'd acted like this, he was psyching himself up to do something nice for me.

No need to catastrophize just yet.

"I found something," he said, drumming his thumb against the steering wheel.

"Oh?"

"I hired a hacker to get information on your kidnappers, and found out they were part of an entire trafficking ring." He kept glancing over at me, gauging my reaction. My expression didn't change at all, as a chill went all the way down my spine, settling into each of my limbs. Freezing me in place. "Members had tattoos of the ouroboros. It's said that they lived by feeding on their own."

"On their own..." I echoed, latching on to the last thing he'd said. On other people like me. People with auras...

It wasn't just me that was hurt by them.

"I'm going to find them and I'm going to make him pay for what they did to you." Mitexi's eyes were like iron. Cold and determined. "If it takes every last cent that I own, I'm going to make them pay."

Mitexi fumbled with the lock for a bit, pausing at the doorknob for a split second, before pulling it open wide.

For a second I'd thought that we'd gone to the wrong address.

I turned back to look at Mitexi, wide-eyed. He looked like a man meeting his date's parents for the first time, like he should be holding a hat in both hands, shuffling the rim around in his grip.

I walked deeper inside, trying to sort through the unfamiliar layout. "But this... this was Chase's room." I stood where his door used to be, and all that was there was a blank wall. Right next to it should have been Will's room, and there wasn't anything there either.

Wordlessly, Mitexi walked to a door that definitely hadn't been there before we'd gone on the trip, and opened it for me.

Inside it was wide and airy. Plush lavender carpet lined the floor, and fairy lights hung in rows from the ceiling, like stars. A television screen covered the entire far wall, and it was currently projecting an image of floating clouds.

In the center of the room was a four-poster bed, with gauzy hangings and more glittering lights—a bed fit for a princess.

It was like stepping right into the middle of a dream.

Mitexi gazed around the room, inspecting every bit of it. Then nodded as if he was satisfied. "The first nest I made for you was too small."

I clasped my hands over my mouth, trying to hold in my gasp. All of my shock.

No, but Mitexi couldn't have.

The room that we were standing in now, used to be Chase and Will's rooms. Maybe even a part of Tycho's room as well. While we were out on our trip, Mitexi must have arranged for the whole place to be gutted and remodeled.

"You didn't have to knock down their rooms," tears filled my eyes. "It was all you had left of them."

"The construction team kept it all. Even ordered display cases for them, and moved it all over. You see, their things have taken over the old nest." A half smile tugged at the corner of Mitexi's handsome face. "It's like I got one of my own."

I shook my head, helplessly. "You didn't have to do this for me."

Now I looked at all of the soft decorations in the room, hating that I loved it.

How could I just come into his space and destroy it? Rip apart all of his last ties to his past? All because of my stupid claustrophobia.

"I did it for them. Because they would have loved you too. Since they aren't here, I have to love you harder. I know it's what they would have wanted."

I shook my head.

This nest was perfect... But I hated that he had to do this.

"But if I wasn't like this, you wouldn't have had to." My words were so soft, as I had to force myself to say them. The thing that I'd really worried about more than anything else.

That Mitexi would see through my pretty facade. That once he did, he would realize that I was broken. That once he saw me clearly, he wouldn't want me anymore.

Mitexi crossed the room, tugging me into his arms. One of his rough hands cupped my cheek, holding me like I was the most delicate and precious thing. Like a flower, or fine china.

"You are enough. Just as you are."

I sniffed loudly, letting his words sink in. As I looked into his stormy eyes, and saw the fiery devotion as he gazed at me, I allowed myself to consider it.

After everything we'd been through... maybe he'd already seen all of those jagged edges within me.

He'd seen it, and it hadn't changed a thing.

I hadn't thought less of him because of all the things he'd gone through. So, why was it so hard for me to believe the same?

I nodded.

Mitexi, my alpha, thought that I was enough.

Reaching for Mitexi, I placed my palm against his cheek. Mirroring him.

"So are you."

THIRTY
PANDORA

I couldn't tell you if I was the one to move closer to Mitexi, or if he shifted into me; maybe we'd simply always been destined to fall into one another's arms. All I knew was that one moment we were gazing into each other's eyes and the next moment our lips had crashed together.

It was the collision of two forces. Of his primal hunger. Of lips and tongue and teeth. Hot and moving together. Building delicious friction that awakened something that was aching within me. A heat in my lower belly.

Mitexi was pressing against me, teasing me. Letting me get just a taste of his arousal, not quite where I needed him. Just out of reach.

I was grasping desperately at his belt, pulling at the leather, releasing it from the notch. Unbuckling and freeing him. Just as he was tearing at my cotton chemise, ripping it open. Groaning, the moment that he realized that I had opted out of wearing a bra —traveling was tough enough without having underwire attacking me for hours—and latching on to my tits. Sucking hard at my nipples, until I was gasping.

He was holding me tight. Refusing to loosen his grip even enough to get my clothes off—they ended up in tatters on the floor soon enough.

Once we were both naked, Mitexi coaxed me to wrap my legs around him. He lifted me carefully onto the center of the bed, which was even softer and more perfect than it looked.

Mitexi gazed at my eyes as he brushed his hands along my cheeks, drinking me in.

"You're perfect. My perfect girl," he murmured, caressing a light trail along my breasts and across my belly. Sending shivers down the length of my spine.

His touch slid down between my thighs, stroking through the slick that was dripping down on the sheets below.

"Fuck," he bit back a groan, as he dipped his finger into me.

I whimpered as he found that spot within me, that made my toes curl and my fists grasp at the bedsheets. He dipped a second finger within me, and all that sweet tension ratcheted up. Spearing me with his rough hands, his thumb circling around my clit, with just the right pressure. Just there.

I gasped, loud. Eyes rolling back as the tension broke apart into bliss.

My walls fluttered around his fingers as I came. Flooding me in pleasure.

Mitexi kissed me, lightly as he pulled his fingers out. Keeping his eyes on mine as he stuck the fingers he'd fucked me with into his mouth. Sucking them down with relish.

"Is my good girl ready to take all of me?" Mitexi's voice deepened into a growl.

"Please. *Please*." My mind was so lost in a post-orgasmic fog, I wasn't even sure what I was begging for, only sure that whatever it was, he had it.

I needed him to give it to me.

Mitexi's eyes darkened, as he took in my pleasured body, stretched out and all ready for him.

He settled himself over me. Lining himself up, notching his thick length against my core.

With one long thrust, he bottomed out within me, until he was balls deep.

My back arched, my head slammed into the pillows at the *stretch*. My walls clung to him, as he dragged against my insides. Filling me with delicious friction.

He felt so fucking good.

I wrapped my legs around his hips, as he began to move. Rocking himself into me.

Again and again. With each thrust he was winding me up just a bit tighter. Driving into me, until all my worries were knocked out of me. Driven straight out of my mind and replaced with friction, with his hot skin, his deep groans, and the rapid slap of his hips into mine, of his balls against my ass.

Mitexi jerked one of my legs over his shoulders, and began teasing my clit as he continued to slam into my pussy. The friction of his rough hands, circling gently right where I needed him most —had me gasping. Desperate. Clutching at every part of him that I could reach. Digging my nails into his skin hard enough to leave marks. Keeping up that perfect pressure... until I burst.

Pleasure pulsed through me, rolling through my body in a wave. Leaving me tingling all over. Until all I could do was lay there, catching my breath.

Completely blissed out.

Mitexi sped up, chasing after his own pleasure. Rocking into me fiercely. Letting go of his control to fuck me like a beast. Like a force of nature.

With a last hard thrust, his whole body shuddered as he came. I could feel him throbbing deep within me. I could feel the warmth of his cum—so much of it—as he filled me with everything he had. As his knot thickened. Pushing against my walls, until we were locked together, bodies intertwined.

Connected with his cock and his cum within me... connected with his bond fluttering peacefully within my mind.

I'd never felt safer in my whole damn life.

THIRTY-ONE

MITEXI

I stared at the alphas in their orange jump suits in the line-up. Turns out that there were six alphas already incarcerated that had the ouroboros tattoo documented in their records.

I looked into each of their eyes. Gauging their expressions to get the measure of these men. Bored. Stoic. Edgy and shrewd.

Was the man who hurt my mate standing there?

Even if they hadn't actually hurt Pandora, had they hurt other omegas just like her?

"Can you tell the men to raise their hands above their heads?" I tilted my head a bit to the side, not taking my eyes off them for a second.

Officer Morris snorted, like this was the punch line of some kind of twisted joke. "Sure, Mitexi. No problem."

I watched as each of them raised their hands. One of them rolling their eyes. Another man just staring at the one-way mirror with a deadpan expression. My eyes darted across their hands, and then zeroed in on the man second from the right.

He had a scar, raised and shiny. Right in the webbing of his hands, between his thumb and pointer finger.

With his hand raised I could also make out the tattoo on his wrist. At first glance it looked like a dark ring. I leaned in closer to the glass to make out the definition of the scales, the slit eyes of the serpent as it swallowed its own tail.

I pointed straight at the man.

"Him."

Officer Morris snapped to attention, narrowing his eyes at the man I singled out. "You sure it's him?"

I had to control my breathing, which was running ragged. All I wanted to do was smash through the glass and wrap my hands around his neck.

The man who'd hurt my mate, and got away scot-free.

She'd had nightmares for years because of this greasy little shit, while he was sleeping easy. Thinking that he'd gotten away with it.

He had no idea what was coming for him.

Officer Morris shook his head. "He's getting released in about two weeks."

"Is his sentence over?" I had to force myself to unclench my fists. To hold them loose at my side.

"No, he's getting out early on good behavior." Officer Morris rubbed at the stubble on his chin, frowning. "Did you want me to have a word with the board?"

I stared at the man.

The man who'd preyed on defenseless omegas and alphas.

The man who hurt so many people, until he'd gone and hurt the wrong one.

The omega who belonged to *me*.

I stared at his hair, greasy and limp. At his wiry frame.

He looked like a stretched out squirrel. Somehow he'd managed to weasel his way into the parole board's good graces, after serving part of his sentence in a minimum security local prison.

Did I want to put my faith in the parole board? Did I trust that he'd repaid his debt to society? That once out, he would never come near Pandora. Never hurt another person ever again.

Slowly, I shook my head no.

"Well then I'm afraid there's not much else I can do," Officer Morris sighed, looking at the line up like he'd look at a half crushed cockroach writhing and stuck on the bottom of his shoe. "Let me know if you come up with anything else. It's the least we could do after that unpleasantness with Daniel. The whole department threw a party—pizza and cake and everything—when we heard that your charges were dropped."

I nodded to Officer Morris respectfully, "Thank you for your time."

I pulled my hat down low over my head, staring nonchalantly through the windshield into the dusk. The time on the dashboard read seven fifteen. It would be any minute now.

The door to the New Oxford county jail opened—fucking finally, and a lone man walked out, rummaging through a clear plastic bag. I started up the ignition, as my heart pounded wildly in my chest.

He opened the door to the cab, buckling himself in without even looking up at me once. Just gave me an address, ignoring me as I started driving.

I watched him in the rear-view mirror. This wiry man. Lean and mean. The worst kind of thug. Watched the thick rings he grabbed out of his bag, and jammed on his hairy fingers. Watched as he fished his cell phone out, cursing.

"Do you have a charger?" He held out his hand expectantly. Still hadn't looked at my face once.

Wordlessly, I dropped the chord into his palm.

He held his phone in a white knuckle grip, staring as the

screen lit up, and the percentage of the charge slowly rose. It had barely reached sixteen percent when he yanked out the chord to make a call.

"I'm out." He held his one hand close to his mouth, speaking in the faintest voice.

I still heard every word.

"Yeah. No, yeah. The parole board is filled with a bunch of stupid cunts... Uh huh. No, I'll be sure to fly under the radar."

He nodded, as if he was receiving directions I couldn't hear, and muttered a quick goodbye.

"Hey, man. What the fuck?" He'd finally pulled his attention away from his phone for long enough to notice his surroundings.

Not that it would do him any good.

He scowled, looking more closely through the windows. Not fiddling with the controls enough to notice that the child-locks were engaged. Just staring at the trees. Too dense for any part of the city or the suburbs.

"You missed my turn."

ABOUT THE AUTHOR

I'm Miyo Hunter and I'm addicted to Dominant Alphas. Sweet love and dark fantasy. From shifters to omegaverse, I want characters bent over chairs and called a good girl. I want to read until jobs and responsibilities don't exist. Until I'm lost in a world that's spicy and a little bit wild.

If you enjoyed reading, please leave a review. Honest reviews help other readers find books that they may enjoy.

ALSO BY ME!

Moonlight Reborn

A fated mates shifter romance, with touch her and 💀, enemies to lovers, and a dominant alpha.

He was the most dominant wolf in the pack and I'm the bullied outcast he hates until his skin touched mine, electricity sparked. Marking us. We both knew what it meant—a soulbond.

Moonlight Trail

A novella MF romance with fated mates, touch her and 💀, and a dominant alpha.

I wished to be a wolf, and what I got was a mate who didn't want me. He was the dark wolf, a dominant alpha, and who was I? I was nothing but a human.

A shifter who'd failed to shift. Will I unlock my inner wolf by the next full moon, and be the mate my alpha would kill to claim? Or will I reject him forever?

Moonlight Shifter — Coming soon!

Finding your soulmate is every wolf shifter's dream—except mine.

I'm already in love. So when destiny revealed my mate, I did the only thing I could. I ran from him. But no matter how strong I am, a lone wolf is vulnerable. When I'm captured, the only one who can come for me, is the mate I'd rejected.

THE POISONVERSE

THE POISONVERSE

Havoc Killed Her Alpha - *Marie Mackay*
Forget Me Knot - *Marie Mackay*
Pack of Lies - *Olivia Lewin*
Ruined Alphas - *Amy Nova*
Sweetheart - *Marie Mackay*
Lonely Alpha - *Olivia Lewin*
And more to come...

Shorts:

His Gold Pack Omega - *Miyo Hunter*
Something Knotty Something Blue - *Lilith K.Duat*

www.ingramcontent.com/pod-product-compliance
Lightning Source LLC
Chambersburg PA
CBHW021333190726
48288CB00003B/1087